D0407112

THE EDGE

ROLAND SMITH

HOUGHTON MIFFLIN HARCOURT
BOSTON   NEW YORK

For Alessia

www.hmhco.com

The text of this book is set in Plantin.

Library of Congress Cataloging-in-Publication Data
Smith, Roland, 1951–, author.
The edge / by Roland Smith.
p. cm.
Sequel to: Peak.
Summary: Fifteen-year-old Peak Marcello is invited to participate
in an "International Peace Ascent" in the Hindu Kush, with a
team made up of under-eighteen-year-old climbers from around
the world—but from the first something seems wrong, so when
the group is attacked, and most of the climbers are either killed
or kidnapped, Peak finds himself caught up in a struggle to
survive, shadowed by the Shen, a mysterious snow leopard.
ISBN 978-0-544-34122-7
1. Mountaineering—Hindu Kush Mountains (Afghanistan and
Pakistan)—Juvenile fiction. 2. Survival—Juvenile fiction. 3. Snow
leopard—Juvenile fiction. 4. Hindu Kush Mountains (Afghanistan and
Pakistan)—Juvenile fiction. [1. Mountaineering—Fiction. 2. Survival
—Fiction. 3. Snow leopard—Fiction. 4. Leopard—Fiction. 5. Hindu
Kush Mountains (Afghanistan and Pakistan)—Fiction.] I. Title.
PZ7.S65766Sh 2015
[Fic]—dc23
2014044086

Manufactured in the United States
DOC 10 9 8 7 6 5 4 3 2 1
4500549221

THE *SHEN*

The snow leopard makes an impossible leap.

Twelve feet.

Maybe fifteen.

Up the sheer rockface.

Landing on a narrow shelf as if she is lighter than air.

Her two cubs stand below, yowling for her to come back down.

She stretches out, her dusky white paws hanging over the ledge. Her long, thick tail flicking back and forth like a metronome.

She looks down at the cubs, yawns, wraps her tail around her body, then closes her pale green eyes.

"THAT'S RUDE!"

"They need their mommy!"

Paula and Patrice. My twin sisters—well, half sisters —the two Peas. Like two peas in a pod. Seven years old. Just. I'm the third Pea. My name is Peak. Not Pete. Peak Marcello.

The two Peas and I share the same birthday. They were born, on the day I turned eight, to my mom and my stepdad, Rolf—a good guy, but very different from me.

Paula was holding my right hand. Patrice my left. We were at the Central Park Zoo in New York City, not far from our loft on the Upper East Side.

"Maybe the snow leopard needs a little break from the kids," I told them.

"Are you saying *you* need a break?" Patrice asked.

"I was thinking the same thing," Paula said.

They look alike, they sound alike, they think alike.

"Lucky for you I wasn't thinking that at all," I told them.

They smiled. Same smile. Same missing teeth.

Different clothes, though. They don't believe in dressing the same. "Twins dressing the same is goofy!" Every morning they have a little meeting and decide who will wear what. No arguments. Fashion is not their thing. Music is their thing.

Piano.

Prodigies.

Both of them.

Me? Not so much. Unless you count the ability to climb sheer rockfaces and buildings a talent. Although buildings are out now or I'll be locked up until I'm eighteen.

"If you can't do the time, don't do the climb."

"What?" Paula asked.

"Nothing." I hate it when my private thoughts come out of my mouth without me knowing it, and it had been happening a lot lately. What was that about?

"You could climb up there," Patrice said, pointing at the mother snow leopard.

She was right. I had already figured out three routes up to the ledge. I couldn't help myself. It's what I do.

"Not as gracefully as the snow leopard," I said.

"There's no snow," Paula pointed out.

"Not in July." It was a sweltering ninety-two degrees in the city and was supposed to get hotter.

"It's still a snow leopard, even without the snow," Patrice said.

"Did you see snow leopards on the mountain?" Paula asked.

She's asking about Everest. I was up there a couple months earlier, but standing at sea level in the sticky heat with the twins, it seemed like a century ago.

"The only animals on Everest are yaks and birds."

"Why?"

"Because there's no food except for camp garbage."

"Snow leopards don't eat garbage," Paula said.

"Birds do," Patrice insisted.

Patrice was right. The birds also picked at the frozen corpses at the higher altitudes, but I didn't tell them this.

"What do they call snow leopards in Tibet?" Paula asks.

I tried to remember. I hadn't picked up much Tibetan or Nepalese on Everest, but it seemed like one of the other climbers called it . . .

The twins' smartphones started playing Chopin's polonaise Op. 53 in A-flat major. The only reason I knew the piece was that they had been practicing it for at least a year. I'd heard the music so many times, I thought I might be able to play it on the piano myself.

"Texts!" they shouted in unison, reaching into their pockets.

That would be *one* text from either my mom or stepdad. They always text all of us so no one feels left out.

Somewhere my smartphone was buzzing too, or maybe not, because I hadn't charged it in a week. In fact, I wasn't exactly sure where I had left the phone. Probably in my bedroom, or maybe in the kitchen. Drove my parents nuts. They couldn't threaten to take it away from me, because I didn't want it in the first place. I understand the idea of smartphones, but I think smartphones look dumb.

Almost everyone in front of the snow leopard cage was holding a smartphone—talking, listening to music, snapping photos, thumbing texts, tweeting, whatever. I'd rather hold the twins' hands than a smartphone.

"Mom," Patrice said.

"She wants us to go to the bookstore," Paula chimed in.

"Right away."

Mom co-owns a small bookstore with a friend.

"*Shen!*" I shouted.

The twins' eyes went wide. The crowd stared at me.

"*Shen,*" I repeated, more quietly. "That's what they call the snow leopard in Tibet."

THE ITCH

MOM'S BOOKSTORE IS called the Summit Bookshop—not surprising, as she was a world-class climber before I was born. But the shop carries very few titles about climbing or mountaineering, and those it does carry are written by climbers she knows personally, including my bio dad, Joshua Wood, whom I rarely see and, to be truthful, don't miss much.

The store was doing okay, considering most people are reading their books on electronic gizmos now. It stays in business because of Mom's taste in books.

When Mom stopped climbing, she started reading—everything. No TV or video games for me, the twins, or Rolf. We spend our spare time with words and music. Oh, and climbing—at least in my case, but not so much since I came down from Everest. Instead, I'd been hanging with the twins, which saved them from hanging out in the bookstore all day. We'd been going to museums, plays, concerts, and movies almost every day.

So far I hadn't gotten the itch to climb, but I knew it was coming. It was just a matter of time.

We left the zoo, walked up Fifth, took a right on East Sixty-Sixth, then walked into the air-conditioned Summit Bookshop. It was jammed with people getting out of the heat. Mostly nannies. On weekday afternoons, the place looks like a daycare center. Mom has a little coffee shop in the corner of the store and makes more money selling coffee and pastries than she makes selling books.

The nannies sipped iced lattes, chattering in several languages over their cooing babies and crying tots, talking about their real children, who lived long subway rides from where we lived. The twins ran over to the strollers and started making baby noises in perfect harmony.

Mom came out of the back room carrying an armload of books with a padded envelope balanced on top. "How was the zoo?"

"Hot, but we were having a good time. What did you need the twins for?"

"I didn't need the twins. I needed you. And knowing you wouldn't have your phone, I used them as intermediaries. I wish you'd carry your phone."

"Sorry."

"Right." She set the books down and handed me the envelope.

"What's this?"

"Vincent dropped it by."

Vincent is my literary mentor, a.k.a. English teacher, at the Greene Street School. The school is filled with little geniuses like the twins. Then there's me. Everyone there has to have some kind of special talent. It was decided, without asking me, that I was the school's writer. To pass to the next grade, I had to write about my experiences on Everest in a couple of Moleskine journals.

I knew what was in the envelope without opening it. I'd

carried Moleskine journals to the summit of the highest mountain on earth—well, almost to the summit.

"Are you going to open it?" Mom asked.

I tore the envelope open. Two Moleskine journals. Blank. Big surprise. There was a yellow sticky note on the cover of one of the journals in Vincent's careful printing.

Write something in First Person Present Tense. V.

"Looks like Vincent has an assignment for you."

"I already completed his assignment on Everest," I pointed out. "And school doesn't start for more than a month."

(Note to Vincent: First person present tense is a ridiculous viewpoint. To start with, it's unbelievable. You're writing as if what is happening to you at that very moment is actually happening right then, but the reader knows that's not true. How can something be happening to you while you're writing about it in a journal? And don't tell me that the writer is merely transcribing what happened in real time. FPPT is a literary trick, but I've used some of it in this journal, so you'll know that I can do it. And I can't believe that you dropped off an assignment a month before school starts. What's the matter with you?)

"It won't hurt you to keep your writing brain working until school begins," Mom said. "You're a good writer."

I wasn't a good writer. Yet.

"Writing is no different from piano," Mom continued. "You have to practice to be good at it."

"Except when you're practicing piano, you're not writing the music—you're playing other people's scores. When you write, you need to have something to write about."

"I'm sure you'll figure something out. But Vincent's assignment is not why I pulled you from the zoo. You have some old friends waiting for you in my office."

"Who?"

"Go see for yourself."

JR, WILL, AND JACK. We'd been on Everest together.

With them was another guy I didn't know. They were gathered in front of Mom's climbing wall. The wall is covered with beautiful photos of her in her former climbing days, clinging and dangling at impossible inverted angles on sheer rock walls along with my real father, Joshua Wood.

"She was called the Fly," I said as I walked into the room.

They all turned around.

"She's incredible," JR said. "It's great to see you, Peak."

It was great to see them, too. We shook hands.

"This is Ethan Todd," Jack said. "The newest member of our team."

Ethan gave me an engaging grin. The name sounded familiar, but I couldn't remember where I'd heard it.

"Ethan is our new tech guy and climbing guru," Will explained.

"Of course," I said. "You're Ethan 'Sarge' Todd. You topped McKinley and rode a snowboard down to the bottom."

"Guilty."

"At the bottom you were chased by a wolf."

"It was a young wolf, and he, or she, wasn't serious—just curious."

"Why do they call you Sarge?"

"Long, boring story."

I liked Ethan, and I was happy to see JR, Will, and Jack. My bio dad had hired them to film me summiting Everest, which hadn't worked out the way my dad, or the film crew, had planned.

"What brings you into town?"

"A couple things," JR answered. "We finished the Everest documentary and signed a distribution deal with ESPN. It airs next month."

"I look forward to seeing it."

"It came out pretty well. You're in it of course."

I wasn't happy to hear that I was in it, but I wasn't surprised. Originally the documentary was supposed to be about me—*the youngest person to summit Everest*—but that didn't happen. I stopped ten feet from the top and videotaped my friend Sun-jo becoming *the youngest person to summit Everest*—but that's another story. It's just as well that it wasn't me. I'd watched some of the tape of JR interviewing me. Awkward is the kindest thing I could say about it. Sun-jo had been much better on camera. "A natural," as JR put it when we were filming on the mountain.

"Remember Sun-jo's interview with the avalanche hurtling down behind him?" Will asked.

It wasn't really an avalanche. The rocks were tumbling, not hurtling.

"Dynamite vid!" Jack said.

I wondered what they were doing at the store. It wasn't like ESPN was across the street. They had to have taken a cab or a subway. They didn't walk. Not in this heat.

"I appreciate you dropping by," I said.

"It wasn't just to say hello," JR admitted. "We have a proposition for you."

"An invitation," Ethan said.

"An opportunity," Jack added.

"What's up?"

"We have another gig," JR said. "Are you interested in a little climb?"

"Is my dad involved?" I didn't care if he was. I was just curious.

JR shook his head. "Have you heard of the Peace Climb?"

Cause Climbs. There are dozens of them every weekend all over the world. Climb for Cancer, Climb for Creatures, Climb for Love, Climb for God, Climb for Whatever, advertised in the back of all the climbing magazines. I'm not against causes, but I prefer to climb alone if possible.

I told them I didn't know anything about it.

"Do you know who Sebastian Plank is?"

"Of course." Sebastian Plank was the richest man in the world, or so it was said. He had his digital fingerprint in a dozen billion-dollar high-tech businesses. Rolf was one of the two-hundred or so attorneys he had on retainer. Our loft was probably paid for by Plank, even though—as far as I knew—Rolf had never met him.

"Plank is sponsoring the climb," JR said.

"Paying for the whole thing," Ethan added. "First class all the way. Private jets, catered food, the best climbing gear money can buy."

I'd always wondered about this worthy cause travel deal. My parents had a lot of friends who spent their free time and money traveling around the world to third world countries for a week or two at a time, planting food, digging ditches, and building houses. It seemed to me that the people they were trying to help might be better off with the cash their friends spent to travel there. Mom says I'm too cynical. She's probably right.

"How many climbers?"

"Two hundred plus," JR answered. "All under eighteen."

"From every country on earth," Ethan said.

"Not quite every country." Jack started counting off the excluded countries on his fingers. "North Korea, Somalia, Papua New Gu—"

"Okay, okay. Most countries."

It didn't matter how many countries were represented, because I wasn't really interested in climbing with two hundred plus, or even two, people.

"I appreciate the invite, but it doesn't sound like my kind of thing."

Surprise and disappointment spread across JR's face. It was the same expression he got on Everest after we concluded one of our many horrible video interviews.

"Plank personally requested your participation."

"Why?"

JR shrugged. "As I understand it, everyone else had to apply for the climb. You're the only climber he specifically requested."

If they had to apply, I was surprised I hadn't heard about the climb. I subscribed to several climbing zines and kept up with a half dozen climbing forums on the web. I didn't remember hearing anything about Plank sponsoring a climb.

"We already asked your mom," Will chimed in. "She said it was up to you."

I wasn't surprised by this. After I had gotten busted for climbing skyscrapers and returned from Everest, she'd been all about personal responsibility and freedom of choice. Her summer mantra was *"You make the choices. You own the consequences."* Although since I had returned from Tibet, I hadn't made any consequential choices.

"This could be the first one."

"What?" JR asked.

I'd done it again. "I was just thinking about choices," I mumbled. "Saying no is also a choice."

They stared at me. Embarrassed, I changed the subject. "I didn't know Sebastian Plank was interested in climbing."

"I didn't know either," JR said. "The assignment came out of the blue a couple days ago. Got a call from his people. Met them at our hotel last night."

"So they're paying you well?"

Will smiled. "A lot more than your dad paid."

"What about the climbers? Are they getting paid?" Not that it would make any difference to me.

"They're climbing for the glory," JR admitted.

"And the gear," Ethan said, dreamily. I knew the look. "Don't forget about the gear. Plank's people showed us the list. It's all top of the line, and the climbers get to keep it."

All climbers are gearheads. Including me. The storage unit in the basement of our building is stuffed floor to ceiling with my gear and Mom's old gear. I'm not even sure what's in the unit anymore, but I know it's not enough. Ethan knows the best way to get to another climber is with the allure of gear. I tried to hide my gear addiction, but it didn't work. Ethan gave me the *gear-gotcha* grin. A gearhead can always pick out another gearhead.

Once again, I changed the subject. "Who's the climb master?" A climb with this many people had to have somebody in charge. Probably more than one person.

JR shook his head. "Don't know. They didn't say, but I'm sure it will be someone well known. Plank can get anyone he wants."

Which got me thinking about who else was being recruited for the climb. I'm not in the elite climbing circles, but because of my mom and dad, I know a lot of climbers who are.

"I assume Sun-jo is climbing," I said. "I wonder if he's climbing for Nepal or Tibet."

"Neither," JR said. "He's not on the list."

"That's weird."

"We thought so too. There's a girl climbing for Tibet. Seventeen years old. I haven't heard of her before."

"Probably Chinese," Will said.

He was probably right. The Chinese think Tibet is China. They wouldn't allow a real Tibetan to climb for peace, or any other cause that wasn't in China's political interest.

"What about Nepal?"

"A boy," JR answered. "Also seventeen. Never heard of him, either. I'm sure they tried to recruit Sun-jo, but he must have passed. I hear he's been pretty busy since his Everest summit. Endorsements, personal appearances, and media interviews."

Which reminded me why I was happy that I wasn't *the youngest person to summit Everest*. I liked hanging out with the twins. I liked going to the zoo.

"Sun-jo is nearly impossible to reach," Jack said. "Everything has to go through Zopa. And you know Zopa."

I don't think anyone really knows Zopa. He's Sun-jo's ex-Sherpa. He's also his grandfather and a Buddhist monk who magically appears and disappears when you least expect it.

For a second, probably because of the gear, I had drifted toward saying yes to the climb. But now, because of the media attention, I was drifting back to no.

"I'll think about it," I told JR, which was a polite way of saying no.

"There isn't much time to think about it," Ethan said. "The climb is next week."

"A climb for two hundred people from all over the world cannot possibly be put together in a week," I said.

JR shrugged. "Plank is famous for getting businesses up and running at lightning speed."

"Climbing is not a business."

"That's debatable," Will said.

He had a point. A lot of climbers, including my father, were in the business of climbing.

"What's the big rush?" I asked.

"Maybe Plank's worried that peace will reign on earth and he'll miss his window of opportunity," Will said.

We all laughed.

"Seriously, though," JR said. "There is a deadline. Plank wants the Peace Climb documentary to air on Christmas Day."

"You're kidding me."

"No joke. He's already bought the airtime. If we don't have the vid in the can by Ho Ho Ho Day, we don't get paid."

That was insane, but I guess if you're one of the richest people in the world, insane is not an obstacle.

"So if I don't climb, who's next on the list?"

JR looked uncomfortable. "Yeah, that's the thing, Peak. If you pass, the U.S. won't have a climber in the mix."

"That's ridiculous. There must be a thousand climbers in the States under eighteen who could do the climb. I could give you names of dozens of climbers right now who would jump at the chance."

JR looked even more uncomfortable, if that was possible. He glanced at the others as if he was asking for their permission. Ethan, Jack, and Will all gave him a nod. JR took a breath and said, "We . . . um . . . we sort of assured them that you . . . um . . . that you would climb if they hired us to film the climb."

I stared at JR, not quite understanding what he was saying.

"Are you saying that if I don't climb, you lose the job?"

"That about sums it up."

"Kind of optimistic, wasn't it?"

"What?" JR asked.

"Assuring them that I would go on the climb."

"I guess," JR admitted. "But there wasn't much choice. I'm not sure they would have come to us if it weren't for our connection to you."

A tenuous connection. Like being fixed together on a frayed rope.

"I'm not convinced of that," Jack objected. "They saw the Sun-jo video. They were impressed."

The Sun-jo video. Would it have been called the Peak video if I had succeeded? Not that I have any regrets. I chose not to reach the summit for a very important reason. But I'd be lying if I said I didn't think about Sun-jo trudging up those last ten feet, imagining myself following in his heavy footprints to the summit or, better yet, Sun-jo following my footprints to the summit.

"There are a thousand videographers right here in New York with more climbing creds than we have," JR said. "They picked us because of Peak."

"It's nice of you guys not to mention the fact that I totally let you down on Everest."

"You didn't let us down!" Will said. "You shot the vid of Sun-jo reaching the top. We used almost every second of it in the documentary. If it weren't for that, we wouldn't have had anything."

I didn't take the video for their documentary. I took it to prove that Sun-jo had reached the summit of the highest mountain in the world.

"I don't understand why Plank's people didn't come directly to me if it was so important that I join their Peace Climb."

"That's a great point," JR said. "We talked about it all the way up here in the cab."

"And what did you come up with?"

"Zip," JR said. "It doesn't make sense."

"Let me ask you this," Ethan said. "If Plank's people had asked you directly, what would you have said?"

I thought about this, but not for long. "I probably would have said no."

Ethan grinned. "Well, there you go. Maybe their approach was shrewder than we think. We've been talking to you for ten minutes, and you haven't said no."

Apparently Ethan didn't understand that *I'll think about it* meant no. But then again, maybe it didn't mean no. Not any longer. Because now I was thinking about saying yes. If I said no, they'd lose the contract. I wasn't sure that I wanted to let them down again. If I said no, I'd probably never find out why Plank wanted me to climb so badly that he was willing to forgo a climber from the USA altogether.

And then there was the gear.

Ethan maintained his grin. "What do you say, Peak? Are you in or out?"

I returned the grin, which I suspected looked a lot like Ethan's.

"In," I said.

The crew visibly relaxed.

JR pulled a folder out of his backpack and gave it to me. "We leave first thing in the morning. Plank is sending a car for us. We'll swing by and pick you up on the way to the airport. We'll be at your apartment building around seven. Your visa is inside."

"Visa?"

"Yeah. And don't forget to bring your passport. You can't get into Afghanistan without it."

I stared at him, trying to wrap my mind around our climbing destination and recalling the titles in the stack of books Mom had been carrying. I wasn't certain, but I thought all of them had the word *Afghanistan* on the spine. I wondered if I would have said yes if I'd known where the climb was taking place.

"Isn't there a war in Afghanistan?"

"Technically, no," JR says.

"What about untechnically?"

"Yeah, there is still stuff going on over there. Skirmishes. Political unrest. Protests."

"Terrorism," I added.

JR shook his head. "I don't think so. Our troops have all but pulled out. I think they have an international peace-keeping force there. Something like that. But we'll be a long way from where the problems are, and we're doing something positive. The risks are minimal. And Plank has hired a private security force to watch our backs just in case."

Mom walked in, still carrying the stack of books. "Well?"

I looked at the spines. I was right about the word. "Is it okay if I go to Afghanistan tomorrow?" I asked.

"Sure," she said, then looked at JR. "I just got off the phone with Plank's people. I'm going with you."

PLANKED

BEFORE ROLF CAME along, Mom and I were together twenty-four-seven because Josh was gone twenty-four-seven. It had been a long time since we'd gone anywhere together, just us. She was sitting across the aisle from me in one of Plank's private jets, sound asleep with an open book about Afghanistan in her lap.

Rolf had been pretty good about the whole thing, considering the twins let him know about it the second he walked through the door from work with . . .

"Peak has to write in *first people presents.* He and Mommy are going to *After Can Stand* on a little vacation, just them, but they'll be back in ten days. We ordered Chinese food for dinner. I'm not eating the *egg food young.* Yuck."

Rolf understood *egg food young* was egg fu yung.

"After Can Stand?"

"That's right. We looked at a map. It's right next to *Pack Her Stand.*"

Reading and diction were not the Peas' strong suit. It took Rolf a few seconds to translate twin-talk into English, and when it dawned on him what they meant, I could see by his expression that he thought he had it wrong. He looked at Mom.

"Afghanistan?"

Mom nodded.

"Tomorrow?"

Another nod.

Rolf poured himself a drink and sat down. "Tell me about it."

It took all of about five minutes for Mom to explain. The twins got bored halfway through, wandered into the music room, and began practicing a duet of Mozart's sonata in B-flat major. I said nothing. Mom's explanation was succinct and to the point. After she finished, even I thought the idea of flying to war-torn Afghanistan in the morning to climb a mountain for a Christmas television special made perfect sense.

Rolf took a gulp of his drink, then a second gulp, before responding.

"Of course you both know that Sebastian Plank, like many geniuses, is nuts."

"You've met him?"

"Twice. He's a little hard to follow when you're talking to him because he talks faster than any other human being on earth, and most of what he says has nothing to do with what he's supposed to be talking to you about. But that's okay because he always shows up with four personal assistants. When Plank leaves a meeting—no more than ten minutes after he arrives—two PAs stay behind for a couple of hours and interpret what he just said. In our firm we call it getting Planked. Other firms call it a Planking."

"So you don't trust him," Mom said.

"On the contrary. Sebastian Plank, as odd as he is face-to-face, is completely reliable. If he says something's going to happen, it happens or it has already happened." Rolf looked at me. "This might be my fault. I may have let the cat out of the bag."

"How so?"

"Plank was in the office a couple weeks ago. He asked about the family. I told him about the twins, the bookstore, and "—he took a breath— "your Everest climb. I told him you stopped just short of the summit to let a friend get the glory."

Mom frowned.

"I'm really sorry, Peak," Rolf said. "It was out before I knew it. I didn't think Plank was even paying attention. I thought he was just being polite."

"No big deal," I said. And I meant it. Sun-jo was still the youngest person to reach the top of Everest.

Rolfe looked relieved. "Did you know about this Peace Climb before the film crew showed up at the bookstore?"

"No."

He looked at Mom. She shook her head.

"I bet nobody else knows about it either, except for his people and the people participating in the climb. This is how Plank works. There'll be some rumors floating around by now because of the Internet and social networking. But the climb will be over before any of the rumors are confirmed. Did they have you sign anything?"

"A nondisclosure agreement," Mom said.

I hadn't signed anything, but at fifteen, my signature wouldn't have been legally binding anyway. I knew this because Rolf was my stepfather. Obviously some of his legalese had rubbed off on me.

"There you go," Rolf continued. "You just got a Planking. It seemed like a last-minute deal to you, but it wasn't. I'll bet you that almost every climber and participant was contacted within a two-hour window. The only odd thing, in Peak's case, is that they sent the film crew to enlist him. But there was a reason for it. Of that you can be sure."

I told him about the film crew's deal being dependent on me agreeing to climb.

"What did I just tell you?" Rolf said. "I guarantee there was a backup plan to your saying no. Probably a plan C and D as well. One of the backup plans, no doubt, was to call me, or someone in our firm, and enlist us to get you to climb."

"Do you want us to pass?" Mom asked. "It's not too late. We don't have to go."

Rolf laughed. "It might be fun to see what Plank's next move would be if you did change your mind, but no, I don't want you, or Peak, to pass up this opportunity." He set his drink down and took Mom's hand. "To be honest, I've been waiting for you two to go climbing together for years. I didn't think it would take this long, and I certainly didn't think it would be in Afghanistan, but the day has finally arrived."

"I'm not climbing," Mom said. "I'm just a technical advisor."

Mom had not climbed since she smashed her leg in a fall years before. She still walked with a slight limp, very slight, from time to time.

Rolf smiled. "Oh, I suspect you'll be doing some climbing. I'm happy you're going. I'd be worried about Peak if you weren't."

The intercom buzzed. The piano stopped. The twins ran to the front door shouting, "Egg food young!"

APPROACH

We are somewhere over the Atlantic. I miss the two Peas, and I've only been gone a few hours.

Mom's not the only one sleeping at forty thousand feet. JR, Jack, Will, and Ethan are behind us with their seats reclined as far as they'll go. They all looked pretty rough this morning when the van swung by to pick us up. They were asleep before the jet took off. Behind them is one of Plank's people. His name is Tony. He's dressed in a three-piece suit. I don't think he's climbing with us. When we got onto the jet, he gathered our passports and visas and has been madly typing on his laptop since takeoff. His skin is pale, like he's never been off the jet. I want to go back and talk to him, but every time I turn to look at him, he's hunched over the machine tapping away.

THE FLIGHT ATTENDANT came down the aisle again, carrying a basket of snack food. His name is Rob. Every fifteen minutes he has offered me the basket.

I smiled again. "No thank you."

"You sure?"

"Positive. I'm stuffed."

"Already? I haven't even served brunch yet. We're having fresh crepes. Five varieties. My favorite is the pesto, cheese, and egg."

"Then I definitely don't need any more snacks. I'll save

myself for a pesto crepe when it's ready. But I do have a question."

"Ask away."

"Is this your first trip to Afghanistan, or have you been here before?"

"This is my second trip in a week."

"This is my first trip," I said. "What can you tell me about it?"

He gave me an odd look. "Virtually nothing. It's strictly touch-and-go for us. We fly into Kabul, refuel, and take off. The next trip will be in ten days to pick you up."

"What about Tony? What does he do?"

"Tony's the man to talk to you about Afghanistan. He's an international travel facilitator. An expert in passport and immigration control. His job is to make certain that when you get off the plane, there are no hassles. He's fluent in Pashtun, Dari, Wazari, and I think Farsi. He's here to grease the wheels, so to speak."

"Who else have you flown into Kabul?"

"An older man last week. He didn't give me his name, and even if he had, I wouldn't be able to tell you what it was. Mr. Plank believes in need to know. All I know is that your name is Pete."

"Actually, it's Peak."

"Really?"

"Common mistake."

"Odd first name."

I nodded at my sleeping mother. "Odd parents."

"That's your mother?"

"Yep, that's Mom."

"She doesn't look old enough to have a son your age."

"When she wakes up, tell her that. It will make her happy."

"I will."

"So do you know what we're doing here?"

"Not specifically, but I gather from the equipment on-board that you are climbers." Rob looked at his watch. "I better get going. You're welcome to go back and talk to Tony."

"He looks busy. I don't want to bug him."

"I'm sure he'd be happy to talk to you. Unlike me, he's been all over the Stans."

"The Stans?"

"Kazakhstan, Tajikistan, Uzbekistan, Kyrgyzstan, Turkmenistan, Pakistan, and Afghanistan. The word *stan* means 'place of.' Tony's parents were British diplomats. He grew up in the Stans."

Rob wandered back up to the galley to start cooking crepes. I wandered to the back of the jet like I was going to use the lavatory, pausing when I got to Tony's seat. He looked up from his laptop and smiled.

"Is everything well, Peak?" he said with a British accent.

"Everything is fine, thanks. Relaxing flight. But probably not for you. You look busy."

Tony laughed. "Don't tell anyone," his whispered, "but I'm playing *League of Legends*."

"What's that?"

He laughed again. "I take it you are not a gamer."

"Not even a little."

"Smart boy. *League of Legends* is an online game that is very addictive and a bloody waste of time, but flying around like this, I have nothing but time to waste."

"Well, I'll let you get back to—"

"I was just bludgeoned to death. Take a seat."

I took a seat across from him.

"I hear you're responsible for making sure we get into Afghanistan without any hassles."

"Yes I am. You are all set. The only small glitch we are going to have is that it appears we will be landing just before afternoon prayers, which could certainly delay things, but only slightly."

I'd just read about these prayers in one of Mom's books. Devout Muslims pray five times a day. *Fajr,* just before dawn. *Zuhr,* noon. *Asr,* afternoon. *Maghrib,* sunset. *Isha,* evening.

"I also understand you were raised in the Stans."

"Indeed I was, but I spent most of my childhood in Afghanistan. My parents worked for the British government."

"Diplomats."

"Not exactly. Mother and Father—long retired, so it is safe to tell you now—were spies."

"You're kidding."

"I am not. And don't be deceived. A spy is nothing like how it is portrayed in novels and films. Their job was to make friends and gather information from them. I'm afraid there wasn't much cloak and dagger to it. They threw dinners and parties, and went to dinners and parties, and I usually accompanied them, along with my sister and brothers. It was a wonderful life. Most of my best friends live in the Stans."

"Do you work full-time for Sebastian Plank?"

"Good lord, no. I'm an independent consultant. I've worked for him six or seven times. Most of my work is for governmental agencies, especially the Stan governments, which have a very short shelf life in that many of them are overthrown on a regular basis. Business has been booming, as you would say in the States, for the last decade."

"I don't know anything about Afghanistan."

"That is nothing to feel bad about. Most of the so-called experts, and I include myself in this small group, know very little about Afghanistan. All you need to know is that the country has been in a state of war for thousands of years. Genghis Khan, Alexander the Great, the British, the Soviet Union, Al-Qaeda, the Americans, the Taliban, and several others, have all attempted to take over Afghanistan."

"Why?"

"Genghis Khan and Alexander the Great wanted the country because of the trade route through the Khyber Pass. The Soviet Union and the British wanted the country as a geographical buffer zone against the Chinese. Al-Qaeda wanted the country as a hideout and training ground for terrorists. The Americans wanted to punish Al-Qaeda for what happened on 9/11. The Taliban wanted, and still want, to turn Afghanistan into a religious state."

"What do the Afghan people want?"

"Most of them want to be left alone, especially in the tribal areas, or frontier, which I assume is where you will be. The frontier is not much different from your Wild West, except that your Wild West lasted only a few decades. The Afghan frontier has been in place several millennia, and I doubt any group, or any country, is ever going to tame it. They have their own ways of doing things, and the people who live there resent outside interference. Afghans are an independent lot. Cantankerous. Tough. Completely loyal to their friends. Utterly ruthless to their enemies. Unfortunately, the only time the tribes and rural villages come together as a people is when someone from the outside tries to interfere with their way of life. When the invaders leave, they go back to warring with one another."

"We're on a Peace Climb," I said.

"So I understand. What does that mean?"

"I don't really know."

"It's been so long since the Afghans have had peace, I'm not sure they know what the word means either. But they are goodhearted people. Like most of the one point six billion Muslims in the world, the Afghans are trying to live a good life, raise their families, and get by. Ninety-five percent of them are great people. The other five percent have a strange take on the Koran. I suspect this percentage holds true for Christians and their Bible as well."

"I read that Afghanistan grows more opium than any other country in the world," I said.

"That's part of getting by. It's a four-billion-dollars-a-year industry with about twenty-five percent of that money going to the farmer and the rest divided between district officials, insurgents, warlords, and drug traffickers. Afghans are poor. Seventy percent of the people in Afghanistan work in agriculture, and the average income is less than five hundred dollars a year. It's not surprising they've turned to growing poppies, but it's ruining the country. Where you're going, you probably won't run into any fields, and if you do, get out of there as quickly as possible. Where there are poppies, there are problems."

"I don't know where we're going," I said. "But I'll be sure to stay clear of poppy fields. Do you know where we're climbing?"

Tony shook his head. "Afraid not. All I know is there will be a helicopter waiting for you at the airport. You'll be flown in to wherever you're going."

CALL TO PRAYER

SEVERAL HOURS LATER, our jet touched down in Kabul. I put my Afghanistan books away as we taxied toward a small private hangar. Rob walked down the aisle for one last check.

"The crepes were outstanding," I told him.

"In ten days I'll make you another batch. You taking those books with you?"

"I was just thinking about that," I answered. The books were heavy, and I doubted we'd have much reading time. "I don't know what else to do with them."

"If you want, you can leave them here. Same crew, same jet will be picking you up."

"That's great. Thanks."

I handed them over and looked out the window. Heat waves shimmered across the tarmac. The jet came to a stop and a ground crew got to work. There was a helicopter parked outside the hangar being refueled. We unbuckled and got up from our seats. Rob popped the door open. A blast of hot air filled the interior like he had opened a furnace door. A man wearing a khaki uniform stepped aboard with a big smile and sweat stains under his arms.

"*Asalaam alaikum!*" He embraced Tony.

"*Wa'alaikum asalaam!*" Tony returned the embrace, then

turned back to us. "This is my very good friend Iskandar. A direct descendent of Alexander the Great."

"Do not listen to this foolish man. I am no such thing. If I were from the loins of Alexander, would I be but a humble immigration police officer? I think not. But we must hurry. *Asr* begins soon."

Tony looked through the doorway. "The afternoon prayer starts when the shadow of an object is the same length as the object itself and lasts till sunset. *Asr* can be split into two sections; the preferred time is before the sun starts to turn orange, while the time of necessity is from when the sun turns orange until sunset. Imams don't look at clocks to calculate prayer times, they look at the sky."

"Tony the Islamic scholar," Iskandar said.

Tony smiled. "Hardly, but I do think we will have time to conduct our business before the call arrives. The paperwork is in perfect order as you will see. All you have to do is sign off on it." He took a folder out of his briefcase and handed it to Iskandar, who made himself comfortable in one of the leather seats.

For all his cheerfulness, Iskandar seemed to take his job very seriously. He examined each passport and attached visas in minute detail. He pointed to JR, Will, Jack, and me. "You were all in Nepal and Tibet at the same time."

"We were filming on Everest," JR said.

"Did you reach the top?"

"One of our climbing party did."

"But he is not here?"

"No," JR answered.

Iskandar looked at Mom, then at me, then back at Mom. "Is this possible?"

"Is what possible?" Mom asked.

"That you have a son so old. You look far too young. Perhaps you are brother and sister."

Mom smiled. "Thank you, Iskandar. You are too kind."

Iskandar looked back at me. "Peak? Is that truly your given name?"

"Truly," I said.

He looked back at Mom for confirmation. She nodded.

"Everything appears to be in perfect order." Iskandar handed everyone their passports. "There is a helicopter waiting outside, but I must caution you. There has been some trouble in the Hindu Kush. Some groups have been operating in the area this past week. I doubt they will cause you any problem because I understand that you will have security in place. Again, it is nothing to worry about, but I would be remiss if I didn't at least mention it to you."

Now we knew where we were going, sort of.

"Thank you for letting us know," JR said. "We'll keep our eyes open."

A sound came from somewhere outside. A mysterious sound. A beautiful sound. We filed out of the jet onto the blistering tarmac. Our gear was being quickly transferred to a battered helicopter that looked like it had barely survived the most recent war, or maybe the war before that. The wonderful sound was the call to prayer. It seemed to come from all around on the hot, dry air.

Tony pointed at a tall minaret, not far from the hangar.

"The airport has its own mosque, or the mosque has its own airport. However you put it, the faithful don't have far to travel to pray together five times a day."

Someone shouted something, and the gear transfer came to an abrupt halt as the ground crew jumped into the back of trucks and took off across the tarmac in the direction of the mosque. Tony and Iskandar headed toward Iskandar's official-looking car with police lights and whip antennas.

"Where are you going?" I shouted after them.

"To pray, of course," Tony shouted back. "I am one of those one point six billon Muslims I was telling you about, as are my sister and two brothers. My parents are Protestants. All of you stay where you are. We will be back soon."

"What's that about?" Mom asked as we watched them drive away.

"I was talking to him about Afghanistan while you were sleeping. His parents were stationed here and in the other Stans when he was growing up." I didn't bother to tell her that they had been spies.

JR joined us. "I was just talking to the helicopter pilot. He's flying us to the Wakhan Corridor. Looks like we're climbing in the Pamirs." He spread a map out on the hood of a truck and pointed.

The Wakhan Corridor is a spit of land in the northeast corner of Afghanistan. It's bordered by Tajikistan to the north, China to the east, and Pakistan to the south. I knew about the Pamirs from my climbing books and magazines.

Most of the articles were nostalgic pieces about how great it was in the Pamirs before the most recent war.

"The name comes from the word *pomir*," Mom said. "It means either 'roof of the world' or 'feet of the sun,' which, depending on your perspective, means pretty much the same thing."

"Where did you learn that?" Mom was always surprising me with bits of arcane info like this.

"Books," she answered. "When they said we were climbing in Afghanistan, I figured it was probably the Pamirs. It's an iconic climbing area, or was, before the war. Where's base camp?"

"Roughly right here." JR pointed at a spot next to what looked like a good-size river. "The pilot doesn't speak very good English, and my Pashtun, if that's what he speaks, is nonexistent. But I gathered that we're the last of the climbers to arrive. He flew another group in early this morning."

I looked at Mom, and she returned the look as if she knew what I was thinking, which was *Rolf was wrong.* If we were the last group of climbers, Plank didn't tell everyone about his Peace Climb at the exact same moment. We were on our way to Afghanistan less than twenty-four hours after we were told. It was unlikely—correction: impossible —that two hundred other climbers beat us to base camp.

"What do you think?" I asked her.

"Something's not right."

"What are you talking about?" JR asked.

"Are you sure there are two hundred climbers?"

"That's what they told me."

"And they didn't tell you we were climbing in the Pamirs?"

JR shook his head. "All they said is that we were climbing in Afghanistan. That when we got to base camp, the film director and climb master would give us further instructions. The secrecy was to keep, and I quote, 'the rumors at bay and the media away.' Sebastian Plank doesn't like getting scooped."

"And I don't like heading into the mountains blind," Mom said, which was a little ridiculous, because we had all agreed to go without knowing exactly where we were going.

"It's not ideal," JR agreed.

"And do you have any idea who the director is?" Mom asked.

"No. But I'm guessing it's someone with a big name. Plank hangs with Hollywood's A list. Now that we know where we're climbing, I'd guess that the climb master is a local, or someone from the outside with a lot of climbing experience in the Pamirs."

Afternoon prayers must have ended, because the pickup truck with the crew was heading back across the tarmac led by Iskandar with his emergency lights flashing.

JR looked at his watch. "I guess all our questions will be answered in about three hours."

The crew got the rest of the gear loaded into the helicopter quickly. As they crammed the equipment into the small cargo hold and behind the seats, Mom grilled Tony about the climb. He knew less than JR, which I already was aware of, but he did pass her questions on to the pilot in Pashtun. All the pilot knew was where he was dropping us off and picking us up. He was in a hurry to take off. He wanted to get back to Kabul before dark.

We piled into the cramped helicopter. The rotors began to spin. Tony backed away, his red tie waving in the artificial breeze.

BASE CAMP

The Hindu Kush. Killer of Hindus. Or so I have read. From two thousand feet, it looks dangerous, stark, beautiful. Desert colors. Browns, tans, rust, with spots of green where water runs . . .

JR WAS BUCKLED into the copilot seat, filming every rise and curve as the helicopter snaked its way up the steep, narrow valleys toward the snowcapped Pamirs. Mom and Will were glued to the right-hand window. Ethan and I were gawking out the left-hand window. Jack was squeezed behind us on a jump seat with his digital recorder going, holding a boom mike, whacking us in the head every time the helicopter turned. I wasn't sure why he had it out. No one was speaking.

I was looking forward to climbing again on a real mountain with real rocks instead of on the brightly colored plastic hand- and footholds at the climbing gym. I was picking out climbing routes up every crag we flew over.

JR twisted around and pointed the camera at me.

Crap.

Ethan leaned away from me to get out of the frame. Jack swung the mike boom and dangled it above my head.

"What do you think?" JR shouted above the roar of the rotors.

My pulse raced. My mouth went dry. I'd forgotten

how I was with a camera in front of my face. Tongue-tied. Terrified. Dumb.

"Uh."

Uh? Say something, you moron! Think about how smooth and relaxed Sun-jo was in front of the lens up on Everest.

"Uh. Well. Uh."

For crying out loud!

"It's rugged and spare, but it has its own stark beauty. I look forward to getting down there to feel the rock under my feet and hands and smell the dust and dirt in the cool mountain air."

Stilted. Doesn't sound like me. Which might be a good thing.

"Perfect!" JR shouted. "Now can you say the same thing with your eyes open?"

My eyes were closed? I glanced over at Mom. She was smiling. It had been bad enough blowing every interview on Everest, but to fail in front of your mother over Afghanistan was worse.

"We're still rolling!" JR shouted. "Battery's getting low. Again. Hurry. Eyes open."

I stared at the lens. My eyes felt like owl eyes.

"It's rugged and spare . . ."

I managed to get through it without a stumble. When I finished, I turned my head to look out the window so I didn't have to look at the lens.

"You couldn't have done that better!" JR shouted.

"Bravo," Mom said.

"You've gotten a lot better since we were on Everest," Jack said.

I'd be lying if I didn't say I was pleased with the

compliments, but I couldn't make myself turn around. I was too embarrassed. I didn't want them to see the flush on my burning face. How could I have forgotten this part of the climbing deal? I just hoped that when we got to base camp, there were better faces to film and more articulate mouths to record than mine. I was certain there would be. My plan was to hide among the other climbers. I wanted to be a climbing body, not a talking face.

Ethan joined me back at the window. The helicopter descended and began following a wide river a hundred feet above the churning surface.

"Glacial melt," Ethan said. "Glad I brought my two-person inflatable kayak."

"What else did you bring?"

"Snowboard and paraglider."

"You're kidding."

"I like to come prepared."

I'd wondered about all of the equipment stuffed into the helicopter. Now I knew.

"Wanna do a little kayaking?"

"I've never been kayaking," I said. "In fact, I can't swim."

"Are you joking?"

I shook my head. "My family didn't tread water. We climbed."

"I met your dad once. Cool dude. Can he swim?"

"I don't know." There was a lot I didn't know about my dad. Most of what I knew of him was from reading his books, or articles about him.

The helicopter went into a hover over a small flat spot

fifty feet from the north side of the river and a hundred yards from what I guessed was the edge of base camp. The reason I guessed it was the edge of camp was that there were only four tents in view. There were a couple of people standing near a campfire, which was odd because it had to be at least ninety degrees outside.

The helicopter landed with a jarring thump. We stayed in our seats until the rotors stopped spinning. The pilot jumped out and slid our door open. I was the last one out.

Mom, JR, Will, Jack, and Ethan were staring at the campsite.

"Maybe this is just a staging area," Jack said. "Base camp must be farther upriver. This is probably the only good landing site."

He said this because all we could see were eight brightly colored tents, twice as many as I saw when we landed, but far short of two hundred plus. Tied up outside one of the tents was a donkey and a camel. The donkey was braying.

One of the men at the campfire started walking slowly in our direction. The pilot hurriedly unloaded our gear by spilling it out to the ground.

"Hey! That's our camera gear! It's expensive!"

"That's my kayak! You trying to punch a hole in it?"

The pilot ignored the protests and, long before the man from the campfire reached us, finished yanking the remaining gear out. He climbed back into the helicopter and, without a goodbye in any language, fired it up. We backed away, and a minute later, it was in the air.

The man from the campfire joined us just in time to

watch the helicopter swing around and disappear down-river. He was wearing a baseball cap, sunglasses, a cam-ouflage camera vest with a thousand pockets, matching camouflage pants with more pockets, and hiking boots. Everything looked expensive and brand-new, which could be a problem, especially the boots. Bad idea to drop into the middle of nowhere with untested boots. He pushed his sunglasses up on his forehead. His white teeth and blue eyes stood out in sharp contrast against his meticulously trimmed black beard. He was sweating.

"Phillip Stockwell." He put his hand out. There didn't appear to be a callus on it. His fingernails were perfectly manicured. And clean. He was not a climber. "You must be my cinematographers."

JR shook Phillip's hand and looked uncomfortable. They were videographers. Documentary makers, not movie guys. I was betting that this was the first time in his life he'd been called a cinematographer.

"I'm sure you've seen my films," Phillip said.

JR looked even more uncomfortable. So maybe it wasn't the cinematographer thing. He glanced at his crew for help. Jack, Ethan, and Will gave him completely blank looks. It was obvious they had no idea who Phillip Stockwell was either.

"Great to meet you," JR said feebly.

Phillip looked at me. "And you must be our final climber, Pete Marcello."

I shook his hand without bothering to correct him. His hand was soft.

Phillip looked at Mom. "And you are?"

"Teri. Peak's mom."

He didn't seem to catch the name correction. "All the other climbers came solo. No parents."

It was hard to believe that two hundred parents let their underage climbing offspring come to Afghanistan solo. I wasn't sure why Mom had decided to tag along, but I wasn't embarrassed about it. She'd been pretty cool, treating me like a fellow climber, not like her firstborn. No nagging. No did you remember to bring, did you forget to, don't do that. I think she was happy to be heading up to a mountain to reconnect with her former self.

"But it's fabulous you're here," Phillip continued. "Cindy will have someone to hang out with here at base camp."

"Cindy?" Mom asked.

"Yes, my um . . ." Phillip turned around. "Ah, here she comes. My PA."

His PA, a.k.a. personal assistant, a.k.a. girlfriend (I guessed), was going to be disappointed if she thought Mom was going to be her base camp BFF. Cindy was wearing python-patterned pants as tight as snakeskin, knee-high red leather boots, and a long-sleeve pink spandex shirt as tight as her pants. She wasn't wearing a hat. She didn't need one with the pile of perfectly coiffed hair on her head. Her makeup was perfect. I wondered if she had a makeover PA in her tent.

"Cindy," Phillip said, "this is our final young climber, Pete Marcello, and his mother, Teri."

"I can't imagine why the United States, or anyone else, ever wanted this country," Cindy said. "It's absolutely prehistoric. Do your cell phones work?"

I hadn't brought my cell phone, of course, and I wasn't sure if Mom had hers either. But the newly crowned cinematographers all fumbled their phones out of their pockets, looked at the screens, and shook their heads.

"I think there are satellite phones in the gear Plank gave us," JR said.

"Don't hold your breath," Cindy said. "There's still no signal. And the batteries are going dead because there's no electricity, or bathrooms, or running water, but we do have a camel and a donkey. All we're missing is the Virgin Mother and a manger."

"The batteries would last a lot longer if you'd stop constantly scanning for sat signals," Phillip told her.

Cindy fixed him with a bright smile that wasn't really a smile. "How do we know there's a signal if we aren't scanning for a signal, love?"

Definitely boyfriend/girlfriend, I thought, and the relationship is on the Wakhan Corridor rocks.

Mom changed the subject. "Where's base camp?"

Phillip looked confused and pointed at the eight tents. "That's base camp."

"We were told there were two hundred climbers," I said.

Phillip laughed. "Here we go again. You obviously didn't get the memo, but don't feel bad—none of the other climbers did either. Plank played this one close to his chest, like he always does, to avoid petty bickering. The two hundred climbers are climbing all over the world in groups of five or six. We will all complete our climbs on the same day, roughly at the same time. You . . . we . . . drew the Pamirs. It was totally random."

"That's not what his people told us," JR said, his face reddening.

Phillip smiled. "Really? What did they say? Exactly."

"That this was a Peace Climb with two hundred young climbers, all under eighteen, from almost every country in the world. The location would not be revealed until we got here."

"Carefully scripted," Phillip said. "That's exactly what the other climbers and film crews were told. Plank did it so people wouldn't start wheeling and dealing. Asking to climb here rather than there, or with this team or that team, this director or that director. You assumed everyone was climbing together, but they didn't tell you that. You filled in the blanks."

JR looked at Mom and me. "I'm sorry."

Mom shrugged. "I guess we all got a Planking. It's no big deal. And Plank is right about the bickering over who climbs where. It would have been a mess if he'd been up-front about it."

So, Rolf was right after all. I was actually relieved there were only a few climbers. I hadn't been looking forward to climbing with two hundred people. Five or six was okay with me. In fact, it was great.

"But you knew about this, Phillip." Cindy said, sharply. "All the directors knew where they were going. You could have insisted we climb somewhere besides this godforsaken place."

Phillip slipped his sunglasses back over his now angry blue eyes. "We've been through this. It was a take-it-or-leave-it proposition. In or out. And you didn't have to come with me."

He walked back toward the tents.

Awkward moment.

Cindy kept the fake smile on her face.

I wanted to tell her that mountains are not godforsaken places. They are where humans go to find God, which is kind of the whole point of humans climbing mountains. But of course I didn't.

Mom tried to break the tension with a cheerful question. "So, where is everybody?"

"I have no idea," Cindy said. "The climbing guru, or whatever they call him, took all the kids for a hike several hours ago. He said he wanted to see what kind of shape they were in, which was ridiculous, because the only one that looks out of shape is him. I bet the guy is a hundred years old. The camel and the donkey are his. Apparently he rode them here instead of taking a helicopter. So there's a good chance that he is a nutcase."

"What's his name?" I asked.

"He was here when we got here," Cindy said. "I didn't catch his name. Short, bald dude with a funny accent. Not very friendly." She looked at Mom. "Anyway, I'm glad you're here. It will be fun to have someone to talk to for the next ten days. About the only thing to do around here is skip rocks in the river. I didn't know what I was going to do when everyone was off climbing. To be honest, our so-called Afghan guards creep me out. All they do is stare at me, or leer, and I'm pretty sure they're making snide remarks, but I don't know what they're saying."

I looked at her snakeskin pants and had a pretty good idea what they were saying. Women in Muslim countries don't dress like Cindy.

"Well," JR began, "Teri here is a world-class—"

Mom cut him off. "I guess we should grab our gear and set up our tents before it gets dark."

Cindy pointed at the campsite. "Phillip's and my tent is the big blue one over there. The Afghan guards will clear the rocks away. Well, most of the rocks. I swear they left some under our tent intentionally to make us uncomfortable. I better catch up with Phillip before his pout gets out of hand. You know how artists are."

We watched her walk away.

"I am so sorry," JR said.

"No worries," Mom said.

This made me smile because "no worries" is one of my dad's favorite sayings (usually when there is nothing but worries, like right then). I wondered if Josh had picked the phrase up from her when they were together or if she had picked it up from him.

"What's so funny?" Mom asked.

"Nothing. Guess we better set up our tents."

She looked up at the other tents. "I'm setting mine up as far away from the artist and his PA as I can get."

"I'm completely with you on that."

There were two large duffels with our names on them. I offered to take Mom's.

"You're my son, not my Sherpa."

She shouldered her bag, and after a short search (and a little mom/son debate, a.k.a. argument) we found a semi-flat spot to pitch our tents, closer to the river and about fifty feet from the other tents.

The two Afghans in camp carried assault rifles slung over their shoulders. It was hard to say how old they were, because both of them had clearly been baked by the sun and dried by the wind for decades. They gave Mom a small bow and shook my hand. Ebadullah and Elham. Unlike Phillip's, their hands were as hard as obsidian. Ebadullah had a black scraggly beard. Elham had a red beard, which had obviously been dyed. I remembered reading that village elders dyed their beards red. I wondered what village they were from. The closest village I'd seen was at least a hundred miles away. A three- or four-day walk.

Both men were wearing traditional Pashtun clothing. Leather sandals, baggy linen pants, kurtas, which were long shirts that hung almost to the knee, and turban caps. They squatted down and watched us unpack the duffels. Our domed tents, one green, one red, popped into place with a single jerk of the main support pole.

Mom laughed in delight. "We didn't have these when I was climbing."

"We still have to pound in the tent pegs the old-fashioned way." I used an ice ax to set the pegs.

With that taken care of, it was climbing gear time. As promised, the gear was the best that Plank's considerable money could buy. And there was plenty of it. The duffels were stuffed with everything anyone would ever need to climb any mountain in the world, including a portaledge, which I had only seen in photographs. A portaledge is essentially a tent that hangs on a cliff wall. If you get stuck by bad weather, or the dark, you attach the ledge to the wall and sleep, or rest, hanging there. I pulled it out of the carrying bag and asked Mom if she had ever used one.

"In my youth, but it wasn't nearly as fancy as this. Your dad and I got stuck on walls several times when we first started climbing, before we learned how to speed climb. We invented our own portaledge, but it was more like a sling than a tent. We once spent forty hours in one of our contraptions, after which we were barely able to move. I think one of the reasons we shattered all of those climbing records was our fear of hanging on walls."

Some of those shattered records still stand.

"Do you miss it?" I asked.

"I just told you I didn't like hanging on—"

"You know what I mean. Do you miss climbing?"

Mom looked at me a moment. "Sometimes. But what I have now, what I do now, raising the twins and you, is so much more important."

"So why did you come?"

"I've been thinking about that. At first I told myself it was because of you. That I wasn't about to let you go off to Afghanistan by yourself. But that didn't ring true. By the time I was your age, I was completely on my own, climbing every day all over the country. My parents had no idea where I was or what I was doing. They knew that if they objected, I would have climbed anyway. So they essentially kicked me out of the nest, which is what I did to you when you went to Everest. I think my motivation in tagging along here was spontaneity. That's something I haven't had in years. Responsibility trumps spontaneity. This was a good time to go, and it might be my last chance for a while. As the twins get older, they are going to need more of my time. And I am getting older. Climbing is a young person's sport. Younger than me, anyway."

I was a little shocked to hear this. Mom rarely talked about how she actually felt, except when I was doing something wrong. "You're going to climb?"

She smiled. "I have all this cool gear. Why wouldn't I climb? I mean, I won't be climbing officially with you for the documentary, but I'm sure there are some pitches an old lady like me might be able to struggle up. And I know what you're thinking. Mom hasn't climbed in years. She isn't in climbing shape. Blah, blah, blah . . ."

That was exactly what I was thinking.

"But for your information, I've been hitting the climbing gym almost every day for the past six months, while you were at school, or while you were sleeping in. I'm in pretty good shape. I don't think you'll be embarrassed."

"More like inhibited," I said.

"Liar. But thanks."

Before I came along, Mom was considered one of the best climbers in the world. There were many who said she was a better climber than my dad, although I doubted Josh would have agreed, or if he did agree, ever admit it to anyone. Climbers are competitive. We can't help ourselves. Now that she mentioned it, I saw that she did look leaner and more cut than she was a few months earlier, which went to show that I didn't pay much attention to how she looked. I wondered if all kids did this. If she were a friend of mine, and not my mom, I would have noticed and said something.

"Wanna go for a hike?" I asked. "See if we can find the others and the climb master?"

"Maybe we should take some gear just in case we see something we want to climb."

"I like how you think."

We stuffed small packs with rope, carabiners, quick draws, harnesses, chalk, belay gloves, flashlights, knives, helmets, tricams, camming devices, hexes, nuts (not the kind you eat), water, and energy bars. Gotta love gear.

Ebadullah and Elham had a short conversation with each other as we slipped into our heavy packs. Ebadullah wandered over to the film crew, fifty feet away, and squatted down to watch their gear sort, which was probably more interesting than our sort because they had camera and sound equipment in addition to the climbing gear. Elham said something to me in what I guessed was Pashtun.

"I think he's offering to lead us to the others," Mom said.

TRYING TO KEEP UP WITH ELHAM was like trying to keep up with someone riding a dirt bike. He moved upriver over the loose rocks, or scree, effortlessly, with his hands locked behind his back, like he was floating instead of walking. We almost had to jog to keep him in sight.

"His backpack is tiny," Mom pointed out.

"I don't think it would make any difference. He'd still walk the pants off of us."

Elham took a sharp left onto a narrow, twisting animal trail and headed straight uphill. His rapid pace didn't alter, and soon he disappeared. We stopped to drink water. I don't think Elham was even carrying water.

"Bet you a dollar that when we get to the trailhead, Elham is napping in the shade of a tree," Mom said.

"You're on." The only reason I took the bet was that I was pretty certain there wouldn't be trees at the top of the trail. Trees and bushes need water, and what lay ahead was as dry as any landscape I had ever seen.

Mom took the lead and set a pretty fast pace herself . . . a pace I could have kept up with, but didn't, because I didn't want to rush. I wanted to enjoy the feel of Afghanistan under my old boots.

It isn't long before she vanishes like Elham. I'm climbing alone. The rocks slip and crumble under my boots. In several places I have to use my hands to catch myself from skidding backwards on the scree. After one of these skids, I pause to catch the view, but what I'm really doing is catching my breath. I see something move a couple hundred feet above me along the cliff face. A flash of dusky white. Elham? His pants and kurta are white, a soiled white, but he couldn't possibly be this far ahead, nor could he be traveling horizontally on a sheer cliff in sandals. I wipe the sweat from my face and shade my eyes against the glare of the setting sun. I wish I'd thought to bring sunglasses and binoculars, both of which Plank provided. I catch the flash of white again. It isn't Elham. It isn't Mom. It's a shen. A snow leopard. It makes an impossible leap. Twelve feet. Maybe fifteen. Up the sheer rockface. Landing on a narrow shelf as if it's lighter than air. Impossible. A hallucination, a flashback caused by altitude, dehydration, sun, jet lag, or a combination of all four. But it isn't. The cat pauses on the narrow ledge and looks down at me. I see its thick tail clearly, flicking back and forth . . .

"You okay?"

Mom had backtracked to check on me.

I pointed up at the cliff. "Did you see him . . . or her?"

"Him or her what?"

"The . . ." I scanned the wall. There was no sign of the *shen*. "I guess I just imagined—"

"I saw," a familiar, but completely out of place, voice said.

Now I really thought I was having an audio hallucination. I turned toward the sound of the voice to confirm that I had officially lost it. Standing up the trail just past Mom was a man.

It wasn't Elham.

Mom turned and looked at the man. "I don't understand. What did you see?"

"A *shen*," Zopa answered.

I translated. "A snow leopard."

THE CLIMB MASTER

Seeing Zopa in the Wakhan Corridor is less likely than spotting the shen on the cliff. As far as I know, he has never been out of Nepal and Tibet, where I last saw him standing on a road in the middle of nowhere as I left my failed climb and headed home. When I asked him, on that lonely road, how he had gotten there ahead of me, which was impossible, he had shrugged, showed his thumb, and said he had hitchhiked. He had also found the time to get rid of his climbing equipment and his Sherpa clothes, shave his head, and put on an orange Buddhist robe. He took me to the airport in Kathmandu and thanked me for what I had done for his grandson, Sun-jo, on Everest. It was the least I could do. Zopa's son, Ki-tar, died saving my father's life on K2. I'm not close to my father, but a debt like that had to be repaid.

THE ORANGE BUDDHIST robe was gone now, replaced by jeans, a T-shirt that had seen better days, a vest, scuffed hiking boots, and a battered baseball cap that looked like he had picked it up out of a ditch. Two coils of rope were slung across his broad chest like bandoliers. White stubble was growing beneath the cap. He'd been away from the monastery for a while.

I am obsessed with the mystery of things. Not solving the mysteries. Observing them. And Zopa was the most mysterious human I had ever met.

"You're the climb master?"

Zopa shrugged.

I almost laughed.

The shrug. This is what everyone does when you ask a question about Zopa, because they don't know the answer. This is what Zopa does when he is asked a question he doesn't want to answer or you ask a question he doesn't think is worthy of an answer.

Of course Zopa was the master for this ridiculous climb in Afghanistan. Who else could it be?

"You've met my mom."

"She is just as I knew she would be. Stronger than you. And much stronger than your father."

Mom was smiling. I wondered if she was aware that this was probably the best compliment she had ever received.

"I must go back to the top to make sure no one has fallen."

Mom and Zopa scrambled up the slope like a pair of mountain goats. I took my time, enjoying the view of two of my favorite people negotiating the steep scree.

Their trail ended at a sheer wall several hundred feet tall. Zopa, Mom, and Elham waited for me outside the entrance of a cave opening big enough to drive a bus through.

"You have light?" Zopa asked, fishing his headlamp out of his vest pocket.

Mom and I pulled out our new expensive headlamps and slipped them over our foreheads.

Zopa pulled off a coil of rope and handed it to Mom. "You will check on the young climbers?"

"I would be honored." Mom slipped the coil around her neck.

Mom and Zopa had never met. She only knew him through what I had written about him on Everest. He didn't know her at all, but somehow he did. Now he was asking her to check on his climbers. Deciding about someone at first glance is so Zopa-like.

Elham pointed to the sky and said something in Pashtun.

To my surprise, Zopa answered him back in what sounded like the same language.

"You speak Pashtun?" I asked.

"Kathmandu is an international city. Many people from many countries."

Typical Zopa answer, which explained nothing. New York City is an international city with many people from many countries, including Afghanistan, and I don't speak Pashtun.

"What did Elham say?" Mom asked.

"He says he prefers to wait outside so he doesn't miss the evening prayer if we are delayed."

We left Elham watching the sun and followed Zopa into the dark cave. I expected the cave to be cool, but it wasn't. It felt like I was walking into a kiln. It smelled musty and close. Fifty feet from the entrance was a dim shaft of light coming from the ceiling. A single rope dangled from the opening to the ground.

"Chimney," Zopa said.

I couldn't see the source of the light, but obviously the chimney went all the way to the top of the cliff. Three hundred feet up. Maybe more.

"The others should have reached the top by now," Zopa continued. "Climb up and meet them. Have them rappel down the north face cliff on the river side."

I put my pack on the ground. "I'll get my ascenders." Ascenders are mechanical devices that slide up on ropes and grab, making it easier to pull yourself up. Plank, of course, had included the newest and best, and I was eager to try them. But Zopa shook his head.

"Not you," he said. "Just your mother." He looked at her. "Do you need ascenders?"

She smiled. "No."

She slipped on her gloves, grabbed the rope, hooked her leg around the slack, and started up like a vine snake, with effortless fluidity. I had never seen her climb. It was beautiful to watch, but it's not cool for sons, or climbers, to express how they really feel.

"Showoff!" I shouted.

Off, off, off . . . echoed throughout the cave.

She smiled down at me, then disappeared behind a boulder. The rope went slack, and a second later it dropped to the ground. She was free climbing.

I coiled the rope and attached it to my pack.

"How are the other climbers?" I asked, but what I really wanted to know was why Zopa didn't want me to climb the chimney.

"One is odd. Two are out of shape. One is pretty good. None are as good as your mother . . . or you."

"I'm not in great shape either."

"We watched you and your mother come up the scree. You looked to be in great shape to us."

"Us?"

"The *shen* and me."

"I was in slow motion."

"Climbing is not a race."

I was never sure if my strange conversations with Zopa were a result of his English, which was actually pretty good, or if he just thought this way.

"I'm surprised to see you here," I said.

"You have to be somewhere."

"But it's a long way from Nepal. A long way from the monastery. I thought you only came out of retirement to get Sun-jo to the top of Everest."

"People offered the monastery money. It was decided that I should climb again."

"Sebastian Plank."

Zopa shrugged. Although I was sure he knew who Plank was, and all the minutiae of the deal.

"So the monastery made you climb?"

"Nobody can make one climb. It is always a choice."

Here we go, I thought. All answers are indirect. Questions are answered with questions. I changed the subject.

"Odd seeing a *shen* here. I saw one a couple of days ago in New York City. In fact, I was looking at a snow leopard at the very moment I got the call to come here."

"Odder yet to see a *shen* in New York City, where there are no mountains."

"It was at a zoo."

"The ghost cat belongs in the mountains."

"Ghost cat?"

"Snow leopard, *shen, sah, barfānī chītā, wāwrīn prāng,*

shan, bars, barys, irves, ilbirs, him tendua . . . it's called many things in many languages, but I like *ghost cat* because it is rarely seen, and not everyone can see it. Your mother did not see it. The other climbers did not see it either, even though it was there in plain sight."

"My mom wasn't in a good position to see it."

"She was in a perfect position. She wasn't looking. You were looking."

It was more luck than looking.

"How long have you been here?"

"Three days. It took me four days to get here from Kabul."

So Zopa was the old guy Rob was talking about on the jet.

"On the camel and the donkey?" I asked.

"Not all the way. I caught rides on trucks and cars. When the road ran out, I rented the camel. I did not need the donkey, but the owner said they were inseparable. If I wanted the camel, I had to take the donkey."

"Why didn't you just take the helicopter?"

Zopa shrugged.

"When did the others arrive?"

"This morning. The film crew is with you?"

"Yes. And you know them. JR, Will, and Jack."

"Good. They are likeable."

"There's a new guy with them named Ethan."

"What does this Ethan do?"

"He's their technical advisor. He's a climber."

"Is he a good climber?"

"I've never seen him climb, but I've read about him.

He's made some righteous ascents. I like him. I think you will too."

Zopa nodded.

"What do you think of Phillip and Cindy?"

Zopa shrugged. Which was a pretty good answer.

"Has Phillip told you where we're climbing?"

Zopa shook his head. "He has never been here before. He has not left camp. He uses his computer to look at topographical maps and photos, which you know are worthless in picking a place to climb."

"He's not looking on the Internet because there's no signal."

"So the woman has said. It is no big thing. I don't think it matters where we climb as long as it is in Afghanistan on the appointed day. I have found some good places."

"Why didn't Sun-jo come?"

"Busy."

"Doing what?"

"Speaking, endorsing gear, making money."

"This might have been good publicity for him."

"He does not need publicity. He needs to go to school. He almost has enough money to support his mother and pay for his and his sister's tuition. Another month, and he will have enough money to keep everyone he loves alive forever without common worries."

"Did he know I was going to be here?"

"He doesn't know anything about this climb. He doesn't know that I am here. I did not tell him."

"He would have come if he had known."

"Which is why I did not tell him."

"He'll be upset when he finds out."

"He will be relieved that he did not know."

"I don't understand."

My not understanding was not surprising, which is part of the Zopa mystery. When I met Zopa on Everest, my father described him as a cagey monk. He said that it was hard to say what Zopa's motivation was for agreeing to do something. Like Plank, Josh had donated money to the monastery to get Zopa to lead me to the top of Everest, but it turned out that Zopa was really leading Sun-jo to the top. *He's not taking you up there just to do me a favor or because I gave money to the temple,* Josh had said. *There's another reason—more likely half a dozen reasons—he agreed to do it. And you and I will probably never know what all of them are.*

"You are a climber," Zopa said. "Your father is a climber, and your mother. I was never a climber. I was a Sherpa. I helped real climbers to the tops of mountains. Were it not for the money, I would not have climbed, nor would have my son, Ki-tar. Climbing was a means to an end, and the end was not the summits. The end was supporting our families. Sun-jo is not a climber. Because of you, he no longer has to climb mountains. So you are correct he would have climbed if he knew you were going to be here, but only because you are his friend."

"He didn't reach the top of Everest because of me," I protested. "He reached the summit on his own two feet."

Zopa shrugged.

"They showed me a list of all the climbers and where they were to climb," he said. "Sun-jo was to climb Kilimanjaro."

Mount Kilimanjaro is in Tanzania. I'd always wanted to climb it and wished . . . I smiled. This was exactly why Plank hadn't told anyone where they were climbing beforehand.

"Of course I crossed Sun-jo's name from the list," Zopa continued. "They were disappointed, but they did not give up. They asked if I would be one of their climb masters. I was not interested, but I did look at the climbs that did not yet have climb masters. Your name was on the list for the Pamirs."

"How long ago was this?"

"A month and a few days."

"They only asked me a couple of days ago."

"I know."

"How did you know that I would say yes?"

"I did not know."

"So you agreed to lead the climb on the off chance that I would say yes?"

Zopa nodded. "But I hoped you would say no. You should not have come. You should not have brought your mother."

"Why?"

"This is not going to be a good climb."

"In what way?"

Zopa shrugged.

"Then how do you know it's going to be a bad climb?"

"A feeling."

Uh-oh. Zopa's feelings were often a lot like reality. He sometimes knew, or felt, things before they happened. All climbs have disaster as a possible outcome, but I had a feeling this was different.

"What kind of feeling?"

"Something violent is going to happen here."

"Maybe you're picking up all the past violence in Afghanistan."

"Possible. That has happened before."

I started to feel a little better.

"So if you thought something was going to turn sour, why didn't you say no?"

"Because I thought you would say yes."

"At first I said no. I wasn't going to come here, until it looked like JR and the film crew would lose the gig."

"Gig?"

"Job," I translated.

Zopa shook his head. "I wish you had said no."

I'd been wishing the same thing until I saw Zopa. "We'll be fine. All climbs are safe if you do them correctly."

"You cannot control nature, or human nature. I can smell a bad climb."

I gave him a grin. "You smelled it all the way from Kathmandu to Kabul?"

Zopa returned the grin. "That is a good question. I have always wondered if you make a climb bad by thinking it is going to be bad ahead of time. It is difficult to know. Climbs go bad by what people do. Climbs go bad by what people think. And sometimes climbs just go bad."

"I hope you're wrong about this one. Why didn't you have me climb the chimney and join the others?"

"So I could talk to you." He picked up his pack and glanced up at the opening. "Your mother has made it through the chimney and is organizing the climbers for their rappel."

There was no possible way he could know this by looking up through the chimney, which was partially blocked, but with Zopa you never knew. I picked up my pack.

"We will take all the packs," Zopa said.

Hauling seven packs between us wasn't going to be easy. Zopa must have sensed my hesitation.

"I will ask Elham to help us," he said.

"Evening prayer," I reminded him.

"Too early for evening prayer. He has plenty of time."

He called Elham into the cave. Apparently Zopa was right about the prayer time because after a brief conversation (of which I didn't understand a word), Elham cheerfully slung a pack over each shoulder.

I followed the cagey monk and the rifle-toting Afghan back out into the light.

THE TEAM

I WAS GULPING water as the five ropes were hurled over the cliff. I offered my water bottle to Zopa. He finished it off. Evening prayer had commenced. Elham was behind us, kneeling toward Mecca on a small prayer rug he had pulled out of his little pack.

The ends of the ropes were curled at our feet like brightly colored snakes, each a different color. The sun was sinking behind the cliff. If the climbers didn't hurry, we'd be heading down the unstable scree to base camp using headlamps.

Zopa and I tilted our heads back and shaded our eyes from the bright sun. Five shadowy figures appeared on the edge with their backs to us. I wondered how Mom was going to handle the rappel. A free-fall race to the bottom, or a synchronized controlled descent? Most climbers, me included, liked the free-fall race.

"We will see who is in control," Zopa said. "The climbers or the climb master."

They pushed off at the exact same moment. Apparently Mom was in control. Synchronized. Which is not that easy, because the cliff routes are all different, even though the climbers are only strung twenty feet apart. They have to pay attention not only to their route but to the rate of descent of the person next to them. Mom was in the middle, two climbers on her right, two on her left. She was controlling the descent with fifteen- to twenty-foot pitches. At first the line was a little ragged, but by midcliff everyone seemed to have caught the rhythm. Push off. Drop twenty. Push off. I'd done synchronized rappels many times, but I'd never seen it from the ground. It was an impressive thing to watch. They all touched down at the exact same moment.

"Nice job!" Mom congratulated them as they unhooked their harnesses and retrieved their ropes.

The climbers were drenched in sweat. They took their helmets off. Three guys and a . . .

My breath caught in my throat. The girl shook out her long, damp black hair and smiled at me. Her eyes were pale blue. Her copper-colored arms were bare and chiseled. My legs went weak, and it wasn't from crab walking across the scree with two packs.

She stripped off her climbing gloves and put her long-fingered hand out. "*Bonjour.* You must be Peak. I am Alessia Charbonneau."

I took her hand. Speechless. This had never happened to me before. I thought I might have had a minor stroke.

"I am a very big admirer of your father and your mother," Alessia said.

She was still holding my hand. Or maybe I wasn't letting go. I hadn't even glanced in the direction of the other climbers since I laid eyes on Alessia, but I could hear them chugging water and murmuring in the background like Alessia and I weren't standing on the same slope, or in the same country. That's when I realized I hadn't said one word to Alessia.

Say something!

"Nice rappel."

Are you kidding me? Nice rappel? That's what comes out of my mouth?

"Your mother insisted," Alessia said. "She wanted to test our control after the difficult climb through the chimney. I thought I would get some rest when we arrived at camp. I did not sleep well last night because of my excitement, but Zopa"—she released my hand; it felt like someone had just cut my rope—"is, how do you say, a task maestro."

"Master. Taskmaster."

"Ah, *oui,* my English is . . ."

"Your English is excellent. My French is, well, nonexistent."

"You know Zopa?"

"Yes." But of course no one really knew Zopa. "I was on Everest with him."

"You were on Everest?"

Her blue eyes got that *look.* It was like I had just said I'd met God. I immediately regretted telling her because—

"You reached the summit?"

I shook my head. I almost met God.

She looked sympathetic, but not in the you-loser-if-I-had-been-on-Everest-I-would-have-made-it-to-the-top sense, which I appreciated.

"Just to be on Everest," she said, wistfully.

"It was great," I said, but in truth, it wasn't that great. It was cold, and there wasn't much air to breathe.

"Zopa was the climbing"—she had to think about the word—"master."

"Technically my dad was in charge of the climb. Zopa

was kind of the lead Sherpa. He's reached the summit many times."

"He did not tell us this. In fact, he did not say anything about his climbing experience."

I wished I'd followed his lead.

"Why did he not have you climb the chimney?"

I wanted to shrug. If any of the other climbers had asked this, I would have shrugged. But I kept my shoulders where they were and said, "He needed help with the gear."

Alessia laughed. "So you were Zopa's Sherpa."

"Who's a Sherpa, mate?"

This came from another climber. He was a little older than me. Australian, by his accent. Apparently Alessia and I were not alone on the mountain. There were other climbers. The spell was broken.

"Peak was on Everest this year too," Alessia informed everyone.

Now I really regretted saying the *E* word.

The Aussie stuck out his huge hand. "The name is Rafe. Rafe Rounder. Why didn't you climb the chimney?"

I shrugged.

"I've been to Everest," Rafe continued, loud enough to be heard in Uzbekistan. "Topped it a few weeks ago. You're Peak, right? Met your dad at base camp. Righteous dude."

"South side?" Mom asked.

He nodded. "Fifteenth to summit."

Mom can spot a liar from ten miles away. There are basically two routes up Everest. The southern route, which is in Nepal, and the northern route, which is in Tibet. We had climbed the northern route. There was no possible way

Rafe could have met my dad in base camp on the south side, in a different country.

"Didn't see you in base camp," Rafe said suspiciously, glancing at Alessia with a slight grin.

There were so many things I could have said . . . *That's because we were on the northern route. You have to be at least sixteen to climb the southern route, and I was fourteen at the time.* Or, *That's because we weren't on the Nepal side, and neither were you.* If we'd had a cell or satellite signal, I could have proved this in about thirty seconds. Everyone who summits Everest is listed, with the time and date of their summit, their climbing group, and their age. I've checked this list every year since I was seven years old. I didn't remember a Rafe Rounder on the list. And it was a short list.

"Base camp was crowded," I said. "A lot of climbers this year."

Mom gave me a smile. Zopa smiled too. Climbers are evaluated by their climbing skills, not by their mouths or past climbs.

"I'll say," Rafe said. "It was like a shopping mall at Christmas. But I'm still surprised I didn't bump into you." He gave Alessia a sly look. It was obvious that Rafe had a crush on her and he was trying to crush me.

I wondered if what Zopa had smelled was Rafe Rounder.

"Enough talk of Everest," Alessia said, to my relief, and introduced me to the other two climbers, Aki and Choma. I don't think they had any idea what had just been said during the exchange about Everest. Aki was from Japan. Choma was from Ukraine. They didn't appear to understand or speak much English, but they had bright, enthusiastic smiles. They were both fifteen or sixteen years old.

"We go now," Zopa says. "Dark soon."

This made me smile. Zopa's English was a lot better than that. Who was he trying to fool? Cagey monk.

We started down the treacherous scree with Zopa and Mom in the lead. Behind them were Elham, Aki, and Choma, followed by Rafe and Alessia, who were walking side by side—not easy on the loose rocks. I suspected, actually I hoped, that Rafe was trying to keep abreast of Alessia and that Alessia was not trying to stay next to Rafe. I followed behind. I'm not sure why, but it seemed like the most comfortable place. At least on this trip. I wasn't feeling the drive that I usually feel during a climb. The scramble. The push to be first. To lead. When you climb alone, you are always in front. And to be truthful, I wasn't feeling my best. I was either exhausted or else I was coming down with something.

Halfway down, we all turned on our headlamps. Two-thirds of the way down, it was pitch-dark. I stopped to readjust my pack and get a drink of water. There was no moon. A million stars hung in the black sky. Seven headlamps bobbed down the scree in front of me. I turned around and looked back at the cliff. I wondered if the *shen* was watching us. When I turned back around, I saw that one of the headlamps had stopped. I'd lost track of which light belonged to who (or is that *whom*, Vincent?). I figured the light belonged to Mom. I was sure she had plenty to say about Rafe and the other climbers, and we wouldn't really be able to talk at base camp. Tents have thin walls. I made my way toward her light slowly so we'd have plenty of space between us and the others. But it wasn't Mom.

"Is all okay with you?" Alessia asked.

"Yeah. Fine. Just hanging back. Thinking."

"About Rafe?"

"Who?" I joked.

"The climber from Australia."

"It was a joke."

"Oh," she said uncertainly.

I guessed the joke didn't translate from English to French. Or maybe people were more literal in France. Or maybe Alessia was simply nice and didn't understand sarcasm.

"I wasn't thinking about Rafe," I told her, which wasn't entirely true.

"He is an oaf."

"He's okay." Now, this was a complete lie, because he was an oaf, but I wanted her to think that I was nice. I was finding it a lot easier to talk to her in the dark, picking my way across the scree, without having to look at her blue eyes.

"You have been climbing a long time?" Alessia asked.

"Since I could walk. And you?"

"Ten years."

"Your parents didn't mind you coming all the way to Afghanistan to climb?"

"It is only my mother and I now, and this was not far for me to come. We live in Kabul. And I'm not alone out here." She pointed toward the lights. "You know Elham, but did you meet Ebadullah in camp?"

"Yes."

"They were sent to keep an eye on me and provide security for the climb."

"I thought they were locals."

"I'm certain they are, or were at one time, but they've been working for my mother since she arrived here."

"What does your mother do in Kabul?"

"She is the French ambassador."

I'd never met an ambassador, or an ambassador's daughter. What do you say to this? I said, "No kidding." Which I guess was marginally better than *wow*.

"She has had this posting for two years now," Alessia continued. "Before this, we were in Argentina. It was there that I really learned to climb."

"Aconcagua?"

"Yes. The Stone Sentinel."

Aconcagua is one of the seven summits, the tallest mountain on each continent. At one time, I wanted to top all seven, but after Everest, I wasn't sure about this goal.

"It is a simple climb," Alessia said. "A walk up, really."

"Twenty-two thousand eight hundred and forty-one feet is a dangerous climb even if it is a walk up," I said.

"Breaking your ankle is the only real danger. It is like this." She pointed at the scree.

She was moving across the loose rocks remarkably well, with a light step. Not unlike a *shen*.

"I saw a snow leopard today when I got here." I couldn't seem to stop myself from trying to impress her, which made me feel a little more sympathetic toward Rafe. She must have thought that all guys were idiots.

"No!" she exclaimed.

"On the cliff face. It was a long ways off. Zopa saw it too." I'm not sure why I added this last part, but I suspect it was because I wasn't sure if she actually believed me about Everest after Rafe's comments.

"I have never seen one in the wild. They are very rare here, but I've heard their population has increased because of the war."

"Why would that be?"

"The war did not touch the Pamirs. The hunters were fighting, leaving the mountains in peace."

"Then I guess this is a good place for a Peace Climb."

"You are very lucky to have seen one. I am climbing next to you, with your luck. If you do not mind."

"I do not mind at all," I said.

SEARCH AND RESCUE

RAFE GAVE ME the stink-eye as Alessia and I arrived at camp fifteen minutes behind everyone else. It was all I could do not to shoot him a victorious she-walked-with-me-not-you-big-jerk grin. There were now two campfires burning. One of them had a water kettle hanging over the flames. Most of the tents were lit from inside, looking like colorful lanterns against the darkness.

"Gather round," Phillip shouted, which was ridiculous because we were all standing within twenty feet of him and Cindy. "Now that we have all the climbers, I thought it would be a good idea to have a meeting to work out what we're going to do."

"But before we begin," Cindy said, "do any of you have a cell signal?"

Phillip tried to hide his irritation—not very successfully. Several people fished their cells out. All of them shook their heads.

"I can't believe this!" Cindy stamped away to their tent and disappeared inside.

"All right, then," Phillip said. "Back to the meeting. This shoot is pretty simple. In a few days, I will be filming your group climb in the Pamirs. The spot will be determined by your collective climbing skills, weather, and other factors.

This is not a climbing competition per se, but in another sense it is a competition. There are teams all over the world climbing on the same day that we are. All of the climbs will be filmed. All of them will get airtime in Plank's two-hour special, but some will get more airtime than others. I want our team to be that team that gets the extra airtime. We've all traveled a long way to be here. It would be a shame to see our climb, or most of it, on the cutting room floor."

"How do we control that?" Rafe asked.

"By stunning filming, interesting interviews, and incredible set shots. You'll notice I have two campfires burning. One is for cooking; the other is for interviews. Beautiful light. We'll start the interviews tonight." He looked at Alessia. "How much airtime you get in the final cut will in large part depend on how well you interview. It's all about story."

It was actually all about how you looked and what you sounded like. I'd been up that wall before, and I wasn't sure I wanted to climb it again.

"What is a set shot?" Alessia asked.

I was wondering the same thing.

"It's a video sequence that may have nothing to do with your primary climb. We'll insert it because it looks good."

"In other words, it's fake," I said. It was out of my mouth almost before I thought it.

"Not at all. You'll actually be climbing. It's just that where you're climbing may not have anything to do with the real climb. And believe me, I know most of the other directors on this project. They are all going to be shooting raw set shots, hoping to get them into the final cut. It's the difference between a minute or a minute and a half of airtime and five or even seven minutes of airtime."

Phillip was obviously shooting for the seven-minute side of this equation.

"Before we left, I managed to get ahold of some top-secret drone images of the area." Phillip gave us a conspiratorial grin. "Don't ask me how, but I have some friends in the Pentagon from some of the films I've directed. And I've found the perfect spot for our first set piece. I've sent my film crew out to scout the location."

I looked around and realized that JR and the crew were not in camp.

"Where are they?" Mom asked.

"Obviously they aren't back yet," Phillip answered.

"How far away was this place?"

"Five or six miles. I expected them back by now, but I'm sure they'll be along soon. No need to panic."

Mom did not look panicked; she looked irritated. With good reason. The Wakhan Corridor was no place to be wandering around at night. Five or six miles on this terrain in the dark could be lethal. The film crew were all fit, but the only one with any substantial climbing experience was Ethan. I wasn't sure how good his navigation skills were in the dark in a place he had never been before.

"Do you have the secret drone images?" Mom asked.

This was a test question. I knew my mom well.

"In my tent, but I don't see how—"

Wrong answer.

"Get them," Mom said.

Phillip gave her a dazzling smile. "You are not going after them."

Mom did not return the smile.

Phillip pointed the smile at us, ignoring her completely. "I guess I should clarify who's in charge of this expedition. That would be me. As the director, I'm calling the shots here. It's not necessarily the job I want, but I'm the most experienced and very good at it. I'm not going to have my climbers running around in the dark like decapitated chickens. We can't afford to have our climbers injured before the climb."

"And if something happens to the film crew before the climb, you will have no video." This little bit of wisdom was from Zopa. "Get the photographs and the topography maps."

No trouble with Zopa's English now.

Phillip attempted to stare him down, which was like trying to win a staring contest with a statue of the Buddha. Phillip lost. He very coolly walked over to his tent and went inside. We heard Cindy screech a few choice words at him. There is no privacy in a camp. Phillip returned a moment later with a stack of photos and a roll of topo maps. We all gathered around him.

"I still think we should just wait," Phillip said, finding the right photo. "Here's the river." He pointed. "Here's our camp. And here's where I sent them."

Mom and Zopa stared at the grainy photo.

"Show me the spot on the map," Mom said.

Phillip impatiently unrolled the maps, found the one he was looking for, and pointed again. "Right here."

"Point out the camp again," Mom said.

Phillip stabbed a manicured finger at the spot.

Zopa shook his head. "No. We are here." He pointed to a spot about three miles upriver from where Phillip was pointing.

"I think you're mistake—"

"I am correct." Zopa cut him off. "I have been here for several days. I will take Teri and Peak with me to find them."

"Whatever," Phillip said. "But you're wasting your time. They'll probably be back here before you get back." He looked at me. "You may want to stick around. I was just about to go through my parameters for the interviews."

"Parameters?"

"Yeah. You're all free to say whatever you want, but there are certain things I'm looking for. It would be unfair not to tell all of you what I need to level the playing field."

"I'll take my chances." I picked up my pack.

"I would like to go too," Alessia said.

Mom shook her head. "We've got this. No sense in everyone going." She looked at Phillip. "What I don't understand is how Plank would provide all of this wonderful equipment and not think to supply us with two-way radios as a backup to cell and sat phones."

Phillip looked uncomfortable. It was the first time his confident demeanor had wavered even a little bit. "Well . . . uh . . . actually, there are two-ways. It's such antiquated tech, I didn't even think to use them. I'm sure they don't have much range. In fact, I'm not sure they're charged. To be honest, I don't even know how to use them."

If Phillip had thought to break them out, no one would

have had to stumble out into the dark to find the film crew.

Mom didn't give him a bad time about this, because she's cool. "Let's get them out and see if they work. The last time I climbed, two-ways were the only tech there was. If they're charged, I should be able to get them to work."

Getting two-ways to work is as simple as turning them on and switching the units to the same channel. But she didn't mention this to him either. Cool Mom.

Phillip went back to his tent, and after another muffled exchange with Cindy, he and she came back out with a high-impact plastic case. Inside were several pristine, very compact, two-way radios held in place by Styrofoam. Mom pulled them out and screwed on the antennas.

"These are nicer than any two-way I've ever used." She fired them up and looked at the displays. "They're all fully charged. They might have a better range than we think." She punched in the same frequency on all the units, then keyed the mikes. "They seem to be working."

Cindy wandered over to the fire. "Are those sat phones?"

"Sorry," Mom said, handing a radio to Phillip. "Two-ways. You're still disconnected."

I smiled. A double entendre. Mom is famous for them. First one she had pulled in Afghanistan. I think. They're subtle. Especially when they're directed at you. No one else seemed to have caught it.

MY CALVES AND ANKLES were killing me.

There is no way to strengthen the weird little muscles you use when you're walking on scree. It's kind of like walking on fist-size marbles. Zopa's headlamp was a hundred feet in front of Mom and me, following a trail that only he seemed able to see.

"You think Zopa knows where he's going?" Mom asked.

"Zopa knows where *you're* going before you know. So, yeah, he knows. How are your legs?"

"They are on fire. How about yours?"

"Charcoal."

"Glad to hear it. I thought it was only me."

I suspected her legs hurt worse than mine. When I was three months old, she shattered her hip and broke her back in a climbing accident, which ended her climbing career.

"Zopa doesn't seem to be bothered," she said.

"That's because nothing ever bothers Zopa."

"How old is he, anyway?"

"Best guess? Six hundred and thirteen, give or take a century."

The two-way chirped. Mom unclipped it. "Go ahead."

"Phillip here. Checking in. Any sign of them? Over."

Apparently Phillip had figured out how to use a two-way radio. Probably remembered it from a movie he'd seen, or maybe even directed.

"No sign of them yet, but we've only been gone half an hour."

"Roger that. My concern is that the old man has misread the drone photos. I doubt he's seen many of them in his life."

Apparently Phillip didn't understand that when you talked on a two-way, everybody could hear you, including the person you were insulting, if he happened to be standing in hearing range. The other thing he didn't understand was that Zopa doesn't need a map to know where he is and where he's going. He has a built-in GPS. He's a Global Positioning Monk.

"What a moron," I said under my breath.

"I didn't copy that. Can you repeat? Over."

I was about ready to repeat *that*, but Mom shook her head.

"We'll keep searching. If they wander into camp, let us know."

"Roger that. Out."

"I think we've had enough of Phillip for one night." She switched the two-way off and stowed it.

I was a little shocked at how calm she was over this whole mess. "I'm a little worried about Phillip," I said.

"I've seen worse. The person you're going to have to keep your eye on is Rafe."

"He's just a jerk. No big deal."

"He's more than that. He's a one in twenty."

"Huh?"

"Back in the day, that's what your dad and I called them. About one in twenty climbers are twisted. Things haven't changed. You'll need to stay clear of him. You handled his Everest lie perfectly. If you become a threat to him, he'll hurt you. He's a terrible climber. On the top of the cliff, I had to reset his harness. He claimed that Down Under they rigged them differently. Aki, Choma, and Alessia know what they are about, although the two boys are not in the best of shape. Rafe is a completely different story. He has eyes for Alessia, and Alessia obviously has eyes for you."

"I seriously doubt that," I said.

"And I'm serious about you watching your step around

Rafe. He's not wrapped tight. He's singled you out as his main competition. Not only for Alessia, but for the climb."

"This isn't a competition."

Mom laughed, and I immediately regretted saying that, because of course it was a competition. When two or more people are climbing together, it's always a competition even if the people are friends, which is why I prefer to climb alone. And even then it's a competition between me and whatever I'm climbing.

"You know what I mean."

"I do," she said. "So, what do you think of Alessia?"

Leading question, and I wasn't going to climb that route. Especially with my mom. I shrugged, then picked up my pace to catch up with Zopa, despite my sore calves and ankles. Zopa said nothing when I joined him. He was walking quickly across the loose rock, his headlamp down. After a hundred yards or so, he pointed at the ground.

"There."

The rocky ground looked exactly like the mile of rocky ground we'd just covered.

"You don't see."

I stared at the ground harder. I saw rocks.

He toed a rock with his boot. "This one. And this one. Both turned over earlier today by someone. You are good at seeing things. Patterns. Things that are not supposed to be there, like the ghost cat earlier. You will need to pay attention on this climb. Closer attention than usual." He shined his light ahead along the scree and pointed. "Tell me where the trail is."

It took me a while to see it, but eventually I saw a clear trail where the rocks had been disturbed. "I see it!"

"Good." Zopa started walking again. "It is easier to see at night with a headlamp because of the shadows the light casts on the rocks."

"It has to be the film crew," I said. "We didn't come this way today, and we're the only people here."

Zopa looked off into the darkness in front of us. "I am not sure of that."

"What do you mean?"

"You don't feel it?"

All I was feeling was my sore legs. "I guess not."

"Someone is coming our way."

"Who? There aren't any villages within a hundred miles of this place. There are no roads, unless you count the goat path along the river as a road. There's no reason for anyone to be out here."

"Perhaps they are coming because we are here."

"Why?"

"Good question," Zopa said. "And I could be wrong. But I still have the feeling that this climb is going to go bad."

"Phillip? Cindy? Rafe?"

Zopa shook his head. "I have led stranger groups."

I laughed. "You're forgetting that Phillip is in charge of the climb."

Zopa smiled. "That is correct. I had forgotten he was the leader."

We walked another three hundred yards with me glancing

back at Mom to make sure she was keeping pace with us.

"There."

"I see the trail," I said.

"Not the rocks." He was not pointing at the ground. He was pointing at a pinpoint of light in the distance. I squinted my eyes. There were two lights. Then three. Then two again, slowly moving toward us.

"The film crew?"

"I presume."

It took us a half an hour to reach them. They looked like they had fallen off a cliff. Jack and Will were covered with bloody lacerations and bruises. They were carrying Ethan on a crude litter made out of sticks and climbing rope. Ethan actually looked better than they did, except for his swollen right ankle, which was either broken or badly sprained.

"I told you we were headed in the right direction," JR said hoarsely through swollen lips. "Got any water?"

He gulped down an entire bottle, then told us what happened. They *had* fallen off a cliff. After several false starts, they finally found the climb Phillip wanted them to scout.

"Huge cliff face."

"A thousand feet."

"More like fifteen hundred."

"Whatever. You can't miss it."

"If you're in the right area, which we weren't for hours, because Phillip can't read a topo map or interpret drone photos."

"The cliff is riddled with caves."

"Looks like a nesting site for giant swallows."

"More like a dragon rookery."

This one was from Ethan strapped in the litter. He must have been a fantasy fan.

"Anyway, it's a nice place to shoot. Dramatic. I have to give Phillip props for that, even though he didn't know where the cliff was."

"So we get there about an hour before dark. At that point, we should have just turned around, but Ethan said we should do a short recon climb. Figure out some of the camera angles. Test the rock."

"Hey! I just made a suggestion. And not one of you objected."

"Whatever. Anyway, we start climbing with fearless leader here setting ropes, and we get maybe fifty feet up when an anchor pops loose."

"Rotten rock. And these guys are thirty pounds heavier than they should be. Lard climbers. Not my fault."

"So we fall off the cliff."

"We didn't fall. We slid. If we had fallen, there would have been four busted corpses at the base of the cliff."

"It was like sliding down the side of a cheese grater."

"Probably took off some of the extra pounds you guys are carrying. Which is a good thing."

"The only thing that's shedding pounds is hauling your worthless corpse across this scree in the dark. By the time we get back to camp, you'll be walking better than us."

All of this ribbing was good-natured. Surviving a fall

always cheers you up, regardless of the pain you're in. Mom shined her headlamp on Ethan's black and blue and yellow ankle.

"It's not broken," Ethan said. "Didn't hear any bones crunching inside. I'll soak it in the river and keep it elevated when we get back to camp. It will be as good as new in a couple of days. My biggest problem is getting dumped on the ground three times now. The next time might be the end of me."

"You're lucky we didn't leave you at the bottom of the cliff for the dragons to devour."

I took a closer look at the litter, surprised that they had gotten this far with it. Zopa shrugged out of his pack and gave it to me.

"I am a Sherpa," Zopa said. "I will carry you."

"Zopa?" JR asked in shock. Apparently he hadn't recognized him in the dark.

"You're the climb master?" Jack asked.

"Zopa from Everest?" Ethan asked.

"Wow, didn't expect to see you here," Will said.

"You can't carry me," Ethan said.

But Zopa did carry him, ignoring everyone's protests, over the treacherous scree, in a fireman's carry across his shoulders, all the way back to camp, without one slip or any rest.

It was close to midnight by the time we got back to camp. Alessia and Phillip were the only ones awake. Zopa set Ethan down next to the fire.

Alessia was concerned and relieved. "Thank God you are back. We were so worried."

Phillip didn't look concerned or relieved. He looked mad. "Is the camera equipment okay?"

"It's all fine," JR answered, slumping down next to Ethan.

"Then why didn't you run ahead and film Zopa carrying Ethan into camp?"

JR looked at him through dull, exhausted eyes. We all looked at Phillip through dull, exhausted eyes. I couldn't remember being that tired, and I didn't carry Ethan on my back or on a litter, and I hadn't fallen off a cliff.

"Run ahead?" JR asked.

"Are you dense? Zopa just came into camp carrying an injured climber around his neck. A dramatic moment, and you didn't film it."

"Oh."

"Don't worry about it," Phillip said, doing a complete three-sixty attitude change, by giving him a smile. "But we can't miss moments like that."

"Yeah, sorry. Did Plank supply us with a big first aid kit?"

"In my tent, but Cindy is sleeping . . . finally. I hate to wake her."

I was speechless. So was everyone else.

Phillip looked at Zopa. "I know it's late and that you're tired, but could you pick Ethan up? All you have to do is haul him into the darkness, then walk back in with him. Same path, just like you did before. But this time we'll have the cameras set up. One next to the fire, one handheld as you're bringing him in. Don't look at the camera or talk. Just act as if the camera isn't there. Easy."

Zopa picked up his pack. "It will be easy, because I will not be there. I am going to my tent."

Phillip's smile vanished. He raised his voice. "We can't do this in the morning! We have to shoot now in the dark when everyone's tired. It won't play when you're rested and the wounds are dressed."

Zopa walked to his tent without a word.

"Okay," Phillip said. "I guess one of you will have to carry—"

"Forget it, Phillip," Mom said. "You're not getting your shot. It's over. And you're not supposed to be filming the film crew. You're supposed to be filming the kids."

Phillip stared at her, red-faced, as if his head was about to explode. "You're not in charge here. I'm in charge. And I know very well what I'm supposed to do. And Pete just missed the preliminary interviews. They were pretty good. I just reviewed the video I shot." He glanced at Alessia. "We have a couple of real stars. Naturals. I'm pretty sure some of what I shot will make it into the final cut. Unfortunately, Pete isn't on video."

"If you had a camera, why didn't you film us coming back to camp?" Mom asked.

Phillip's face turned redder, if that was possible. "I tried to reach you on the two-way. If you had answered, perhaps I could have filmed you coming back to camp. Why didn't you respond?"

"Must have been out of range," Mom lied. "I'm going to get the first aid kit."

"I told you that Cindy was asleep."

"I'll be quiet. Oh, and my son's name is not Pete, it's Peak. *P-E-A-K.*"

"What kind of name is that?"

Mom grinned. "His name."

PEACE

I open my eyes and see bright red. It's warm. I look at my watch. 10:32 a.m. Late. My legs hurt from the scree. My shoulders hurt from hauling packs. A girl is laughing. It could be Alessia. I've never heard her laugh. I'm hungry. I crawl out into the sunlight. It's cooler outside my tent. A breeze is coming up from the river . . .

MOM WAS STANDING next to the fire, talking quietly with Ebadullah and Elham. Apparently they spoke English as well as Pashtun. I heard the laughter again. It was coming from the river. Cindy, but a very different Cindy. She was wearing a red tank top and shorts. She was sitting on a flat rock, dangling her feet in the water, and looking like she was enjoying herself. Sitting next to her, also soaking his feet, was Ethan. Uh-oh. No one else was awake.

I joined Mom at the fire. Elham and Ebadullah were not speaking English or Pashtun. They were speaking French. So was Mom. Fluently as far as I could tell.

"You speak French?"

"Obviously."

"You never told me."

"There are a lot of things I never told you."

Elham handed me a mug of strong, hot tea.

"Do you speak any other languages?"

"A couple," Mom answered.

My next question should have been, which ones? But I didn't go there. I was impressed that she had held this back. I thought I knew everything about Mom. I was glad I didn't.

"Cindy seems to be in a better mood today."

"Ethan is working his charm, which is not going to make this camp any happier. This could get ugly."

"You mean uglier?"

"Exactly."

"Have Ebadullah and Elham told you what they're doing out here?"

"French embassy. Bodyguards to Mademoiselle Alessia Charbonneau, daughter to the ambassador. In fact, I just spoke to the ambassador."

"The sat phones work?"

"They worked for a few minutes. Long enough for Ebadullah and Elham to check in and for me to tell the ambassador that her daughter is doing fine. Then it went out again, which is not unusual in this area, according to Elham and Ebadullah."

I looked toward the river. "And Cindy missed the window?"

"Afraid so. I was about to tell her we were back in business when the signal failed. We were just saying that it would probably be best to keep our brief sat blip between us. Otherwise Cindy will spend the entire day fiddling with the phone and draining Phillip's battery further than it already is."

"Speaking of Phillip." I pointed.

Phillip had just stumbled out of his tent. His hair was sticking up all over the place. He looked like he hadn't gotten enough sleep. He walked over to us, rubbing his eyes.

"Have you seen Cindy?"

Mom pointed to the river. Cindy laughed and punched Ethan in the shoulder.

Phillip scowled, then looked at the mugs we were holding.

"Is that coffee?"

"Tea."

"I need coffee. I want to head out in an hour. Wake Zopa and tell him to have everyone ready to go. We'll be spending the night at the cliff they scouted yesterday, so you need to bring your gear. With his bum foot, Ethan will have to stay here. I want you to take his place as the film crew's climbing advisor."

He stamped back to his tent.

"Trouble," Mom said.

"Bonjour!"

Alessia stepped out of her tent, waving, with a happy smile on her beautiful face. Unlike Phillip, she looked like she had slept quite well. When she was halfway to us, Rafe caught up with her. It was obvious that he'd scrambled out of his sleeping bag as soon as he heard her. His hair looked worse than Phillip's. He was wearing shorts, and his T-shirt was on backwards and inside out. He said something to her in French. *Am I the only one that doesn't speak French?* She laughed. I hoped it was polite laughter and not that she really thought he was funny.

"G'day, mates! Glad to see you made it back in one piece. I was done in last night. Didn't even hear you come back to camp."

Cindy let out another peal of giddy laughter.

Rafe looked down at the river. "Who's that with Cindy?"

"Ethan Todd," I answered.

"You mean Sarge Todd, the bloke who claims to have taken a snowboard down McKinley?"

I nodded. "Chased by wolves at the bottom."

"Not bloody likely. I have a friend who was there and said that none of it was remotely true."

I was surprised Rafe didn't claim to have been there himself.

"What was your friend's name?" Mom asked.

"Nobody you'd probably know. Bill Weathers. He said that Todd made the whole thing up. Why's he here?"

"Part of the film crew," I said. "Sprained his ankle when the crew fell off the cliff they were scouting. He's out of commission for a couple of days."

"Too bad," Rafe said, clearly not meaning it. "I should have gone with them. You have to be careful around here. I probably could have prevented the fall. This is no place for amateurs."

The film crew were not professional climbers, but they weren't amateurs, either. They'd climbed all over the world carrying extra gear no pro would ever carry.

"Guess we'll never know if this Ethan can climb or not." Rafe grinned and looked at me. "You missed the preliminary interviews last night."

"I heard."

"They went great. I think Phillip's picked his stars." He looked around camp. "Where is Phillip?"

"He's getting ready to leave," Mom said. "We're spending the night at the shoot. He wants to be on the move in an hour."

"I can be ready in ten minutes. Can't wait to get some climbing in." He looked at Alessia. "I'd be happy to help you with your tent and gear."

"No thank you."

Atta girl, Alessia.

Rafe looked at the fire. "Is that tea in the billy?"

"The what?" I asked.

"The kettle, mate."

"Yeah."

Rafe grabbed a mug and helped himself.

Aki and Choma stepped outside their tents and started stretching the night kinks out. Ethan and Cindy started making their way to the fire. Ethan had his arm around Cindy's shoulder, using her as a crutch. Both of them were grinning when they reached the fire. Cindy looked totally different with a genuine smile on her face.

"I'm Ethan Todd, or what's left of him." Ethan stuck his free hand out to Rafe. "I got a little banged up last night."

"Bad luck, mate." Rafe gave Ethan's hand an unenthusiastic shake. "Guess you'll be missing the climb."

"I heal quickly," Ethan said. "I wouldn't count me out. The wheel's better than it was last night."

"Right," Rafe said. "But you won't be going with us today, mate. Not on that."

"That's right." Phillip had returned. He was frowning at Ethan's human crutch. "If all goes well tonight, we'll be back tomorrow afternoon. You'll have to hold the fort down here for a couple of days on your own."

"No problem. I'm happy to stay and—"

"You can't possibly expect him to stay here alone," Cindy said. "He's injured."

Phillip's frown deepened. "Everyone is going to the cliff."

"What about Elham and Ebadullah?"

"They go where we go. Security."

"I'm not a climber or security," Cindy said. "Someone needs to stay with Ethan."

"There's no need," Ethan said. "I'll be fine on my own."

"You're my PA," Phillip said, with his eyes still on Cindy.

Everyone rolled their eyes, including Cindy.

"I'm staying," she said.

It was obvious that Phillip knew he'd lost this battle, and probably his girlfriend as well. He gave her a malicious grin.

"Suit yourself. Have any of you seen Zopa? I roused everyone else, but he wasn't in his tent."

Everyone shook their heads, looking a little surprised. I'd often seen Zopa disappear at inopportune times on Everest. He was always climbing the mountain, but not always with us.

"I'm sure he'll turn up," I said. "He tends to wander off. He'll be there when we need him."

Phillip looked at his watch. "Well, I need him now." He looked at Mom. "I want to leave in twenty minutes. Think you can get everyone moving in the right direction? I need to direct breaking camp."

"But we're not really breaking camp for several days," she said.

Phillip took a deep breath. "Dear God, give me patience. Of course we're not breaking camp permanently today, but on the day we break camp, the weather might be lousy, or something else might go wrong. We need to get our shots when we can, not necessarily in chronological order. When the video airs, it will look like first-person present tense. I'll make that happen in the editing room. Not here. We're shooting raw video. The shots are like words. We'll use the shots to tell a story. It takes hours and hours of film to make five minutes of actual air time . . ."

I smiled. For the first time, I kind of liked Phillip. Vincent would totally understand what Phillip was saying. It was exactly how Vincent explained the writing process.

Phillip continued talking to my mom. "Let's get moving. If Zopa shows up, he can lead the group to the cliff. If he doesn't, you'll be leading them, providing you know where it is."

"I know where it is, but I'm a little concerned about Zopa. We might want to—"

Phillip raised his voice. "This is not summer camp! You're not a bunch of little kids. We have a limited amount of time to pull this thing off. We're not waiting on Zopa or anyone else. Let's get moving!"

Everyone got moving.

"What are you smiling about?" Mom asked when we got to our tents.

"Phillip. I think he just took charge."

"You can't tell people you're in charge. You have to show people, and I guess that's exactly what he just did, but I'm still worried about Zopa."

"He disappears," I said. "He'll show up when we need him."

"Where do you think he is?"

I shrugged. But I noticed that the camel and the donkey were no longer tied up outside his tent.

ZOPA HAD NOT RETURNED by the time we left camp. Cindy and Ethan stayed behind. Phillip didn't say a word to either one of them that I saw. I told Ethan to tell Zopa where we were headed if he happened to return, which was probably unnecessary. Zopa would know where we were going. He always did.

JR, Jack, and Will recorded our every move and word under Phillip's direction, which meant they had to run across the scree to get in front of us, film us passing, then run ahead again, covering twice as much ground as we were, with heavier equipment. Not easy after falling off a cliff the night before.

(Note to self: *Do not become a videographer.*)

But they didn't complain. It was as if the project was fueling them with superhuman endurance. Phillip seemed to have come into his own too, making suggestions for shots, asking us interview questions as we walked. I think having Cindy dump him, if that was what she'd done, had reminded him what he was there for. He was actually smiling from time to time, telling everyone they were doing a great job. Rafe tried to hog Alessia, but every time Phillip caught him doing this, he broke them apart, making Alessia walk alone or with one of us. I'd caught a couple of Alessia's answers to Phillip's questions, and it was clear to me who was going to be the star of the show.

When the cliff came into view, Phillip slowed us down because he needed to pick out what he called the "long shot." I wasn't sure what he meant by this, so I asked JR.

"Phillip hasn't told you what he's doing yet?"

"No."

"I don't think it's a big secret, and it's kind of cool. You're all going to be spending the night on your portaledges. Each of your ledges is a different color. He's going to string you out on the cliff face in the shape of a"—he hesitated—"an inverted *V*. Once you're all set, you'll light up your ledges one by one in order. He had custom letters made that will attach to the ledges. They spell out *P-E-A-C-E,* with the *A* at the top. Jack's going to take the long shot somewhere back here. Will and I will be on the face, along with your mom and Zopa if we need them. That is, if Zopa shows up. We'll be doing the close shots on the cliff face."

It did sound kind of cool, but I wondered why he used the term "inverted *V*," when it was clear that Phillip intended to set up a little mountain. And who was going to be the *A*? Who was the peak? But I didn't ask, because I didn't really care. I was just happy to finally be able to use a portaledge.

Ethan's description of the cliff was perfect. It did look like a dragon rookery, or like a giant had blasted the face with a humungous shotgun. We headed toward a patch of green at the base of the cliff. The green meant moisture, maybe even a small stream. Jack dangled the mike boom in front of my face. JR and Phillip joined him. JR with a camera. Phillip with a tablet. I stopped walking.

"No, Peak," Phillip said. "Keep walking."

I couldn't believe he got my name right.

"I'm going to ask you a few questions. Remember, this is your climb. The adults aren't in it. It's just you and the other young climbers. Just act natural. You're talking to a friend, or if it feels better, you're all by yourself in the Afghan wilderness talking to yourself."

I'd rather not talk at all.

"This is a Peace Climb," Phillip continued. "Obviously every sane person wants peace. We want the senseless killing to stop. We're in Afghanistan, a country that has been at war for centuries. Most of the people here have fought their entire lives, as have their parents and grandparents, and *their* parents and grandparents. My question to you is why do you think wars happen?"

I kept walking, saying nothing, expecting Phillip to give me another prompt or to tell me to hurry it up. He did neither. He just walked along with me, JR, and Jack at his side, silently, camera running.

"Money, religion, land, and power, or a combination of these things, causes wars. It's interesting that some of our former enemies, Britain, Japan, and Germany, are now our friends. So what was the point of all the people who died in the Revolutionary War, World War I, and World War II? Wouldn't it have been better to just skip the war part and get to the friend part? We have to protect ourselves. We have to help those who can't protect themselves. But beyond those two reasons, I don't get the whole war thing."

I walked on for a few more feet with the camera and mike boom in my face, wondering if I should say something else, but I had nothing more to say.

"That's a wrap!" Phillip finally said, grinning. "Beautiful. I loved it."

JR and Jack were grinning at me too. I didn't want the compliment to feel good, but it did. They wandered off to interview someone else. I continued across the scree, thinking about Zopa, the climb, and the twins. I wondered how the two Peas were doing without Mom, which stopped me in my tracks. If I was missing the twins, Mom had to be going crazy. This was the first time she'd been away from them for more than a night. I turned around. We were spread out across the scree for at least a half a mile. Rafe was the closest to me. Mom was a hundred yards behind him. She was walking with Alessia. Behind them were Phillip and the film crew, heading toward Aki, Choma, Ebadullah, and Elham. If I waited for Mom, Rafe would catch up with me, and I might have to walk with him, which I didn't want to do. I turned back to the cliff. I knew it wasn't a race, but I really wanted to get there before Rafe.

I set a brutal pace, and by the time I got there, I was panting like a dog. A tree was being fed by a spring about ten yards across. The water was deep. If Ethan had been there, he'd have been swimming. If I could swim, I'd have been swimming. I got down on my knees.

"Don't drink the water."

I nearly fell in. Zopa was sitting on the far side in plain

sight, but he had been so still when I walked up, I hadn't seen him.

He laughed. "Where was your mind?"

"And where were you this morning?" I snapped back, a little ticked off at being startled.

"Here waiting for you," Zopa answered calmly. "How is Ethan?"

"He won't be climbing for a few days. Cindy is staying in camp with him. Don't you sleep?"

"Not in the way you do."

Big surprise. I didn't recall seeing him sleep on Everest, either. But a lot of people don't sleep on Everest. Not enough oxygen.

"We're spending the night here. Did you bring your gear?"

Zopa shrugged.

"Did you bring the camel and donkey?"

Zopa nodded.

"How did you know that this was where we would be?"

This elicited another shrug. In other words, he wasn't going to tell me, or else he didn't know why he had come here.

"We're using our portaledges to make a mountain on the cliff face," I told him. "It will look like a Christmas tree lit up at night."

I was pretty sure Buddhists didn't celebrate Christmas and wondered if Zopa even knew what a Christmas tree was.

"Come around here," he said. "You are shouting."

I wasn't shouting, but it probably sounded like it to

Zopa, who rarely raised his voice above a whisper that you could somehow hear twenty feet away. I walked around the spring and sat down next to him.

"Is the water really bad?"

"I drank a little a few hours ago, and I'm waiting to find out. I think it is probably good, but I would give it more time."

"So if you start puking, we shouldn't drink the water."

"Correct. But you can take your boots off and soak your feet. You will need your feet the next few days."

My feet were in pretty good shape from walking around New York with the twins, and I had brought my best hiking boots and climbing shoes. I took my boots off, stripped off my socks, and put my feet in the pool. It was shockingly cold.

"Snowmelt from higher up," Zopa said. He pointed to the pockmarked cliff face. "The caves are all shallow. They go nowhere. No escape."

"Escape from what?"

Zopa shrugged.

"How do you know they're shallow?" The caves started two hundred feet up from the base. It was impossible to see into them from the ground.

Zopa pointed. "Look."

It took me a while, but I finally spotted the silver anchors glinting in the sun. There must have been thirty or forty —the cliff face was peppered with them.

"You set all those anchors?" Which was kind of a stupid question, because who else would have set them? I was amazed that one person could explore the caves and set that many anchors by himself in a single day, or a half a day.

"I assumed that Ethan is a good climber," Zopa said, ignoring the question. "I was worried after his report about the condition of the rock. I found some good rock. Solid. Good anchors."

"You should have waited. It wasn't safe."

"It's not safe to climb skyscrapers in New York on your own either."

My former pastime. I didn't know that Zopa even knew about this. Sun-jo must have told him.

"I don't do that anymore."

"I am happy to hear this. Who wants to die falling onto a busy street? I set the anchors because it was faster to do it myself. And doing it myself assures that it was done correctly. You and Alessia are the only good climbers. I didn't want anyone to get hurt."

"How do you know this is where Phillip wants to film the portaledges?"

"He will film here now because the anchors are set."

FIFTEEN MINUTES LATER, the others began arriving in twos and threes. Alessia and Rafe were first, which meant that Rafe waited for her or that Alessia caught up with him.

"Zopa!" Alessia ran over and plopped down next to him. "We were worried about you."

Rafe acknowledged Zopa with a frown. Apparently he was jealous of anyone sitting next to Alessia, even old missing Buddhist monks. He looked up at the cliff. "Easy climb. As soon as I get a drink of water, I'll show you how to put up your portaledge, Alessia. I've done it dozens of times."

"No need," Zopa said. "We won't be using them."

"Not according to Phillip, mate."

"He will change his mind."

"In your dreams. Phillip's calling the shots. It's his show. He's the director."

The *director* arrived at the spring next with Aki and Choma, with the film crew and Mom right behind them.

"Nice of you to join us, Zopa," Phillip said.

The truth was that we were joining Zopa, but I didn't say anything. Zopa was more than capable of defending himself or, in this case, not defending himself, because he didn't respond to Phillip's jab.

Phillip looked up at the cliff face, then back at the group. "We'll take a fifteen-minute breather here, then hike along the base until we find the right spot. We're going to have to pick up our pace if we expect to have everyone in place by nightfall. You've no doubt heard what I'm going for by now. Five portaledges in an inverted *V.* Two climbers on the right, two on the left."

"In other words, a mountain," Rafe said.

Duh, Rafe.

"I guess," Phillip said.

"Who's going to be on top of the mountain?" Rafe asked, nullifying the whole idiotic inverted *V* thing, which I'm sure Phillip had insisted the film crew use if they had to describe the shot to us. I was kind of glad Rafe had outed Phillip on this dumb description.

"It's no big deal who's on top," Phillip said.

"Cool," Rafe said. "In that case, I volunteer."

Phillip shot him a smile, which we had all learned was

probably not a good sign. "It isn't as simple as that. I've got to think about the whole segment and how everything will flow. I've already decided the positions."

"Okay. Who's in the top spot?" Rafe was not going to let this go, and it wasn't going to go his way, or Phillip would have told him that he was on top. I wondered if he would stick to Alessia like glue when Phillip announced that she was on top.

Phillip gave him a resigned sigh. "All right. Bottom right, Choma. Bottom left, Aki. Second right, Alessia. Second left, Rafe."

And that left Peak on the Peak, which I couldn't have cared less about. "I'm fine with Rafe taking the top."

"That's not up to you," Phillip said. "Red is on top."

Red? Then I remembered that my portaledge was red. So was my tent and pack and almost everything else inside the pack. Plank, or maybe Phillip, had color-coded us. Alessia was the green climber. Rafe, yellow. Aki, blue. Choma, orange.

"Seems to me you would want the best climber of the bunch on top," Rafe said.

Mom rolled her eyes. "It's just a set shot. No one is going to be up for an Academy Award."

Here we go. But Zopa put a stop to it.

"We will not need the portaledges."

"Of course we're using the portaledges," Phillip insisted. "That's why I had Plank provide them. I have the letters *P-E-A-C-E* to attach to them."

Zopa pointed up at the cliff. Everyone looked up, but like I had at first, no one appeared to see the anchors.

"We're not climbing here," Phillip says. "We'll scout the cliff for the perfect spot. I knew it would take a while. That's why I wanted to leave base camp early."

"Anchors," Zopa said.

Everyone looked again.

Mom spotted them first. She started pointing. "There. And there. And there."

Everyone looked at Zopa.

"You set anchors in the darkness?" Alessia asked.

Zopa shrugged.

He couldn't have possibly set that many anchors on a rotten cliff face after sunrise. Even Rafe looked impressed. But not Phillip; he was frowning. He wasn't a climber. He had no idea how difficult and dangerous this had been.

"Waste of anchors and time," he said.

"If you find a better place, I will retrieve the anchors and meet you there," Zopa said. "But this is the best place, as you will discover."

I hadn't noticed, but Alessia had taken off her boots and was soaking her feet. Rafe was staring at her feet.

Phillip shaded his eyes and stared up at the cliff in silence for a few moments, then looked at JR. "What do you think?"

"It's close to where we tried to climb yesterday and nearly killed ourselves. I'd hang on any anchor Zopa set. And to be honest, the entire cliff face looks pretty much the same to me. I don't think it matters where we climb. If we use his anchors, it will save a ton of time, and it'll be safe."

Phillip turned back to Zopa. "What do you mean we don't need portaledges?"

"You can use the tents inside the caves. Your peace letters will fit on the tents?"

"I suppose."

Zopa pointed at the wall. The angle of the sun caused the anchors to shine like little mirrors. "Find the middle anchors. Above them is an eagle's nest. See the sticks in the opening of the cave?"

Phillip shook his head.

"Wait."

Ten seconds later, maybe twelve, a huge eagle swooped in and landed on the edge of one of the caves.

"Twenty-five feet down from the eagle cave is another cave," Zopa continued without giving anyone an opportunity to ask him how he knew the eagle was going to return to its nest at that exact moment.

"So?" Phillip said.

"That is the top of your mountain. There are two more caves below on either side. A perfect *A,* or mountain." Zopa looked at me and smiled. "Or Christmas tree. Set your tents in them. Plenty of room. It is more interesting if your climbers are camped in caves than hanging on a wall. More natural."

I think Plank missed the boat with the Peace Climb. A better topic for a documentary would be Zopa. Phillip stared back up at the cliff as if he was considering Zopa's brilliant plan. Alessia's bare foot touched my bare foot. I was surprised I could feel it, because my feet were numbed by the cold water.

"Okay," Phillip finally announced. "We'll use the caves."

Alessia's bare foot was still touching my bare foot.

Phillip and the film crew headed out to scout the shots. Rafe lumbered over to us and sat down on the other side of Alessia. He took off his size-thirteen hiking boots, then peeled off white socks as big as grocery sacks and put his feet into the water.

"Tepid," he said. "I thought it would be cold."

I'm not drinking the water.

Alessia's bare foot is still touching my bare foot.

THE EAGLES' NEST

"Test your radios," Phillip says.

He's just given us the frequency we are to use. It's early after-noon. The sun is well above the cliff.

"I want a synchronized climb up the wall. Zopa and Teri will be spotting from down here. Peak will be in the middle, so every-one needs to pace themselves to him." He looks at me. "Don't go too fast. If you see someone lagging, slow down. I'm shooting for a straight line with blue and orange reaching their caves first, green and yellow next, and red last. There will be a lot of pauses on the way up to allow the cinematographers to get in and out of the frame for tight shots and sound."

In other words, the climb is going to take about a thousand times longer than it would if we weren't filming it . . .

"OKAY. ON THREE . . . two . . . one . . . roll film!"

I started up. Just like the rappel the day before, we were all climbing the same wall but along different routes, each with its own challenges. The climbers to my left were look-ing up and to their right. The climbers to my right were looking up and to their left. I was looking up, left, and right. If I had been on a gym climbing wall, this would have been relatively easy. On a rotten wall in Afghanistan, it was nearly impossible. The other problem was my hands. My legs and feet were in pretty good shape, but my hands were soft. Within fifteen feet, I had several cuts.

"Okay," Phillip barked over the radio. "Drop down; we'll do it again."

We did it again five more times, and each time it got a little easier, because each of us knew the route.

"That's a wrap! Good job, people! Just hang where you are for some tight shots with the film crew."

It wasn't a *wrap* as in *we are done filming*. The tight shots took longer than our synchronized start. A lot longer. At our present pace, I figured we'd reach the caves in three days. JR was filming me, Alessia, and Rafe. Rafe always smiled and struck a climbing muscle pose when the camera was pointed at him. Alessia used a more neutral expression and never posed for the camera. When the camera was on me, I was certain I looked irritated. A climb that should have taken twenty minutes took nearly four hours, or in my case, five hours, because after everyone else got to their perch, I was attacked by an enraged eagle.

I was shocked at how big an eagle looks when it's trying to knock you off a vertical wall of rotten rock. On the first pass, it hit me with its wings.

"Whoa! Missed it!" JR shouted.

I was dangling by one hand. After three flailing tries, I found a narrow chink with my free hand, saving myself from falling to my death on the sharp scree hundreds of feet below.

"I'm going to swing to the right so I can get a wide shot," JR said.

"A wide shot of what?"

"Of the second attack."

"I don't think there will be a second attack."

"Oh, yeah there will," JR assured me.

JR swung out on his rope and caught the edge of a cave thirty feet to my left, then heaved himself into a sitting position on the lip. It was an impressive and dangerous move. I wondered if he would have attempted it if there hadn't been the possibility of getting a shot of me being peeled off the face of the cliff by a bird of prey.

I looked behind. JR was right about me getting hit again. There were now two eagles and they were both circling back toward me. I looked up. My cave was still thirty feet above me. Below, Alessia and Rafe were already setting up their tents. I thought about rappelling down to Alessia's cave and waiting for the eagles to calm down, but as pleasant as that would have been, there wasn't time. I needed to get up to my perch before sunset. We had used most of our daylight during the slow ascent. Plus there was a good chance that the eagles wouldn't settle down until we were off their cliff.

"I'd get scrambling."

Mom. On the radio. She and Zopa were three hundred feet below, shading their eyes with their hands and looking up. Phillip was standing next to them with a pair of binoculars. I knew what he was hoping for.

"Move. Or brace yourself for impact."

Duh, Mom. I couldn't free up a hand to answer her. I scrunched up as best as I could on a vertical wall and shoved my face into a narrow crack to stop my eyeballs from getting plucked out. I felt the air from the first bird's wings a second before it smashed into my helmet. This was followed by another hit on my pack, much harder than the first.

"That was outstanding!" JR shouted.

I didn't take the time to call him a jerk. I started scrambling up before the next attack.

"Zopa says the birds don't like your red helmet and pack," Mom said.

A lot of good that did me. I couldn't dump the pack. My tent and gear were in it. Without the gear there would be no *A*.

"He says the birds have completely ignored the other climbers."

Bad luck for the red climber, I thought. Rafe probably had his fingers crossed, hoping I'd get scraped off.

"Peak! Slow down, man! I need to film you reaching your cave!"

Sorry, JR. Not happening, man!

I started climbing faster. Just as I made it to the lip of my cave and began pulling myself up, I heard an eagle scream. A second later I was slammed in the back. My helmet bounced off the lip. I fell backward and was barely able to prevent a fall by jamming my index and middle fingers into a crack. I'm sure Mom was having a heart attack. I thought I might be having a heart attack. I grabbed a rotten rock with my free hand. The rock crumbled into rust colored chalk. I grabbed another rock. It held, thank God, or the Buddha, or whoever. I pulled myself up to the lip again, got a knee up, then . . .

Bam!

The second eagle hit me in the butt. I flew into the cave,

smashing my face on the back wall, which was only six feet from the opening. I scrambled to my feet, shrugged out of my red pack, tore my red helmet off my head, then leaned out of the cave and waved so Mom knew I was alive. Alessia, Rafe, Aki, Choma, and the film crew were all leaning out looking up at me.

"I got the butt strike," JR said over the radio.

Great. I unclipped my radio. "If you put it on YouTube, I will kill you."

"Roger that," JR came back, then laughed.

"I'm not kidding."

Alessia's voice came over the radio. *"Are you okay, Peak?"*

It was good to hear her voice. It was good to hear anyone's voice.

"I thought I saw blood on your face."

I wiped my hand across my face. There was blood. Quite a bit of blood.

"I'm fine."

I looked out from my perch. The eagles were still circling, but they no longer seemed interested in me.

"Okay, people."

Phillip. Only he called people "people."

"Let's put that little excitement behind us and get back to the shot."

Oh, yeah, Phillip? You weren't up here being attacked by eagles.

"You all need to get your tents up so we can get an idea of where to put the cameras. I need the film crew down here for a meeting. Pronto."

Pronto? What was the matter with him?

I keyed the radio. "Peak here. If it's all the same to you, I'd like to wait until after dark before I set up my tent. I think Zopa called it right about the eagles being ticked off over the red."

I saw Mom and Zopa talking to Phillip. The film crew were rappelling down the cliff. Pronto.

My radio crackled.

"Uh, yeah, Peak. Phillip here. I'm not convinced it's the red that got them excited. I think it might be your proximity to their nest, which is about twenty-five feet above your current position. Do you copy?"

Actually, if I had leaned over the ledge, I could have copied it without a radio. He was standing a hundred yards away and almost shouting into the radio as if I were deaf.

"Yeah, Phillip. I got that. I'm still going to wait until after dark to set up my tent. Don't want to risk having it shredded before you get your shot."

This was followed by a long radio silence. Blood was dripping onto my lap from a cut on my chin. I rummaged through my pack for the first aid kit.

"Roger that, Peak. But as soon as it gets dark, set up your tent. Everybody else? Get your tents up pronto, so we can start framing the shot. Put them as close to the edge as possible. And make sure your letter is clearly visible. You can move the tents back from the edge after the shoot."

I pulled all of the gear in as far as it would go and leaned against the back wall. There was a small mirror inside the kit. The slice on my chin was deep. If I'd been in the city, I'd have gone to the hospital and gotten a couple of stitches. But I was in a shallow cave in Afghanistan. No stitches. I managed to cinch the slice together with butterfly bandages.

How'd you get that scar?

Attacked by an eagle in Afghanistan.

I was kind of looking forward to that exchange.

There were at least two hours before nightfall. I couldn't say the cave was cool, but there was a slight breeze drying my sweat, which made me feel cooler. The adrenaline from the near fall was quickly replaced by sheer exhaustion. Phillip and the other climbers were chattering away on the two-ways. I switched my radio off and closed my eyes.

SURVIVOR

I open my eyes. I see stars against a black sky. Cave. I'm in a cave. The temperature has dropped by several degrees. I look at my watch. Ten o'clock. I've been asleep for five hours? Why didn't they wake me? Why is it so quiet? I turn the radio on, expecting to hear Phillip shouting at me to set up my red tent. But there is nothing. I check the battery. It's fine. I key the mike . . .

"GUESS I FELL asleep."

Silence.

"This is Peak."

Silence.

"Copy?"

Silence.

I scrambled to the ledge. The wall and the ground were as dark as the sky.

"Yo! Can anybody hear me? My radio isn't working."

Silence.

I wondered if I was having a nightmare. I touched my chin. The butterfly bandages were still in place.

"Is anybody there?"

Silence.

How could twelve people simply vanish without a trace? Impossible.

I spent another five minutes shouting.

Nothing.

I put my headlamp on. I still had a short coil of rope. It wasn't long enough to get to the ground, but it was more than long enough to reach the other caves. The only problem was that it was pitch-dark. I couldn't see the ground. I couldn't see ten feet below my cave. The sane thing to do would have been to wait until morning, but the situation was crazy and called for insane action. I tested the anchor Zopa had set on the lip of my cave, ran my rope through, then lowered myself into the dark.

I went to Rafe's cave first, because his was the easiest to get to. His yellow tent was still up. The only thing inside was a small lantern hanging from the roof pole. His pack and gear were gone. There was a white *E* attached to the outside of the tent facing toward the cave opening. By sticking my head out over the edge of his cave, I could see now that all of the tents were lit from the inside.

P-E-C-E.

The bright letters gave me an idea. If everyone disappeared the moment I fell asleep, which seemed unlikely, they would just be getting to base camp, providing that was where they were going. The point was, they might have been able to see the lit tents from wherever they were. I looked at Rafe's lantern. Of course it was the best that money could buy, and of course it had an emergency strobe mode. I switched it on, hoping that if I got all four tents flashing, they'd know I'd been in their caves, that I knew they had vanished.

It took an hour to check the other three caves. Tents. No gear. Nobody home. All the caves were shallow. No back doors. The only way out was to climb down the wall using Zopa's anchors.

Zopa.

It wouldn't have surprised me if Zopa had left me stranded in a cave. I expected odd behavior from the mysterious monk. But Mom would never have done this. Not in a million years. If there had been a problem with the radios and they had to suddenly leave, she would have scaled the cliff in the dark, unprotected, to reach me.

If she were able to.

I had seen the word *dread* a thousand times, but until that moment, I had no idea what it really meant. It felt as if someone had kicked me in the stomach. For a moment I couldn't move. I thought I might puke.

Breathe.

I was no good to anyone if I was scared out of my mind.

Move.

I was in Aki's cave. Blue *P.* His rope was still fixed to the anchor at the entrance. I tested it by jerking on it as hard as I could. It was solid. I snapped it into my harness, leaned back, and stepped into the black void, taking short hops, five or six feet at a time, making sure of my footing before pushing off again. I reached a second fixed rope in less than five minutes. I wasn't sure if Zopa had set the anchor. I tested it before hooking on, which got me thinking about why the ropes were still there. You don't leave hundreds of dollars' worth of rope hanging on a wall, even if you didn't pay for the rope. When I got to the bottom of the cliff, I hoped that Mom and the others would run up to me and ask where I'd been. But no one came out of the dark. The base of the cliff was as empty as the caves. To mask my disappointment and fear, I retrieved the ropes and tied as many of them to my pack as I could. That done, it was time to look around and see if I could figure out what had happened to everyone.

I started where I had last seen Mom, orienting myself by the bright blinking *P-E-C-E* above. It was easy to find, because smashed on the rocks in thousands of pieces were what looked like every two-way, cell, and sat phone. I stared down at the broken plastic.

Someone is coming our way, Zopa had said. It looked like they had arrived. Nobody in our group would have smashed the phones and radios.

I walked over to the spring. I wish I hadn't.

Ebadullah and Elham are lying next to the cool water.
Their throats are slit.
The fronts of their kurtas are covered in dried blood.
Their beards are caked in gore.
Their eyes are open in surprise.
Their rifles are gone.
Their prayer rugs are unrolled.
They were murdered during isha.

The only dead people I had ever seen were on Everest. They were frozen. They didn't look real. They looked like marble statues. Ebadullah and Elham look like dead people. I turned away, stifled a gag reflex, and sat down on the cool ground. Actually, I collapsed. My legs wouldn't hold me. I barely knew Elham and Ebadullah, but no one deserved to be brutally murdered while praying.

What if others had been murdered? Mom. Zopa. Alessia . . .

This got me back on my feet. I began to search.

The backpacks had been ransacked, the contents strewn all over the ground, but the packs were gone. The only things that seemed to be missing were the food, headlamps, stoves, a few ropes, and the film crew's cameras and recording equipment. Everything else was left behind.

I searched the area around the spring. No more bodies. The others had been taken. I'd slept through an abduction. Now what?

I looked up at the cliff. *P-E-C-E* flashed over and over again. It could probably be seen for miles.

Mistake. What was I thinking? That everyone just wandered off and left me alone? If our group could see the flashing letters, the kidnappers could see the letters. They might be headed back to the cliff right now.

I scanned the dark scree for lights. No one could traverse the loose rocks without headlamps or flashlights. It was difficult enough during the day. I didn't see any lights, and was thinking that I was probably safe, when I heard a sound behind me that nearly put me on the ground again. A scream. It wasn't human. I whipped around and came face-to-face with a wet pair of camel lips, bad breath and all, which did put me back on the ground again—not the breath, unpleasant as it was, but the bellowing face in the dark. It wasn't being aggressive. I think it was happy to see me. The donkey trotted up behind the camel and started braying.

"Stop!"

To my shock, they both stopped.

"That's better."

I got to my feet and readjusted my pack. The camel still had its halter and lead on. There was a broken branch tied to the end of the lead. I untied the branch.

"You're free now."

The camel just stood there looking at me.

"Oh, I get it. You want the halter off so it docsn't get tangled."

I'd never taken a halter off an animal, or put one on for that matter, but I'd been working with rope my entire life. How hard could it be? I reached up to unbuckle the contraption, trying to stay clear of the camel drool, then hesitated. The camel seemed pretty calm, docile, cooperative. Somewhere there was a saddle. I might be able to use the camel to haul . . .

There was another sound, and it wasn't the camel or the donkey. It had come from the base of the cliff. I held my breath and listened, and heard nothing.

Just my imagination. I'm just a little freaked—

The sound came again. A moan. I forgot all about the camel and headed toward the cliff. It took me several minutcs, and several more moans, to find the source. And I couldn't have been more disappointed.

"Hey, mate," Rafe said weakly, blinking up at my headlamp.

"What happened?"

"I need water."

He needed more than that. He needed a doctor. There was a four-inch gash on his forehead, his nose was broken, his left ear was torn, his upper lip looked like he had bitten through it, and these were just the injuries I could see. He was lying in some bushes about a hundred feet from where they rappelled down from the caves.

I dribbled a little water into his wrecked mouth, then asked him again what had happened.

He ignored the question.

"How do I look?" he asked, reaching for his forehead. I stopped his hand before he messed with the scab and started bleeding again.

"You look fine," I lied. "Where is everyone?"

He didn't answer right away. I thought he was going to pass out, but instead he took a deep breath and whispered, "Kidnapped."

"By who?"

"Five or six guys. Afghans. Guns and knives. I think two of them were our so-called guards, Ebadullah and Elham."

"Ebadullah and Elham are—"

"More water."

"Sure."

I decided not to tell him about the throat slitting. Plenty of time to let him know about that later. It took almost a half an hour and several more doses of water before I got the whole story out of him, or at least what he knew of the story.

He and the others were in their tents, the letters all set, waiting for sundown, when they got a call on their two-ways from a voice they didn't recognize, saying they would kill Mom, Phillip, Zopa, and the film crew if they weren't on the ground with their packs in three minutes. Rafe looked out from his cave and saw the captives on their knees at the base of the cliff, hands tied, knives to their throats.

"We didn't have a choice. If we hadn't rappelled down, they would have killed them. Water."

I gave him another sip of water. "Why didn't they take you?"

Rafe looked away. "I fell. Bad rope."

Bad rigging was more like it.

"I fell thirty feet," he continued. "I hit the scree."

It looked like he had scraped the cliff face as well.

"Is anything broken?"

He shook his bashed-up head. "I was a bit out of it after I hit the ground. One of them came over to me. I thought he was going to shoot me."

More likely slit his throat.

"But he just left you," I said.

"I guess. I can't remember exactly. He seemed in a hurry to get out of there."

"Were the men on foot?"

"I think so."

"Did you hear a vehicle or a helicopter?"

"Nothing like that. They tied everyone up, then took off across the scree on foot. I tried to follow them, but only made it this far. I must have passed out."

He wasn't far from where he did his header. He was banged up pretty badly. I suspected that he crawled over to the bushes to hide himself in case they came back, then passed out. I didn't blame him. In his condition, I might have tried to hide myself too. He was in no shape to pursue a bunch of guys with guns and bloody knives. Neither was I, but that was exactly what I was going to try to do after I figured out what to do with Rafe.

"Can you sit up?" I needed to figure out the extent of his injuries.

"I dunno, mate."

"Let's give it a try."

I took his hands and pulled him slowly up. He reached for his forehead again. I stopped him.

"Why do you keep doing that?"

"Because you have a gash on your forehead, and I don't want you to open it up again. I think you've lost a lot of blood. It would be best to keep what you have left inside your body."

"What's it look like?" he asked.

"It's not bad," I lied again. The truth was, it looked hideous, as did his ear, lip, and nose. "But you have to be careful with head injuries. I'm going to clean the scrape up and bandage it."

"You called it a gash before," Rafe said.

At least his mental facilities were working.

"I meant scrape." I needed to get him off this subject and cover the gash so he didn't make it any worse than it already was. "The only thing I'm worried about is concussion and broken bones," I said. "But like you said, there don't appear to be any broken bones, and you're not slurring your—"

"My lip feels swollen."

"A little." His upper lip was bigger than the camel's upper lip.

"And my ear. It hurts."

"Just a nick." Actually the earlobe was missing.

I took off my pack and found the first aid kit, which was going to have to be resupplied after I finished with Rafe.

"Do you have a mirror in there, mate?"

I did have the mirror I had used to look at my eagle wounds, but I wasn't about to give it to Rafe. "Afraid not. Sorry."

It took me twenty minutes to disinfect and bandage him. When I finished, he looked like the mummy from down under, although there wasn't much I could do for his tooth-pierced lip and missing earlobe.

"That does it. Let's see how you do on your feet."

"What for, mate?"

"I beg your pardon?"

"I'm perfectly comfortable right where I am. All I need is a sleeping bag to lie on. I need to get some shuteye. Plenty of time to try my legs out tomorrow morning."

"I'm not waiting until daylight to go after them," I said.

"What do you mean, after them?"

Maybe his brain was more scrambled than I thought. "My mom has been kidnapped," I said slowly. "And our friends. We need to do something."

"You're kidding, right?"

I shook my head.

"They had guns and knives. Ebadullah and Elham must have planned the whole thing from the beginning. There's nothing we can do. They're long gone."

"Elham and Ebadullah are dead," I told him. "They're lying next to the spring with their throats slit. They were murdered while they were praying."

It must have taken a moment for this to sink in, because he didn't say anything for a long time.

"All the more reason not to go after them," he finally said. "The men who took your mom and the others are serious bushrangers. If I wasn't banged up, I might consider it, but . . ."

I walked away while he was still talking, mostly because he was making some good points, and I didn't want to hear them. But his excuse that he was in bad shape was bogus. He wouldn't have gone after them under any circumstances.

It took me a while to cool down. I spent the time sorting through the discarded gear for anything useful. Except for the rope, there was nothing I needed. I walked over to the spring. I wasn't looking forward to what I needed to do there, which was to search Elham and Ebadullah for weapons and phones. It was an unpleasant job, and it yielded zero. When I finished, I covered them with their prayer rugs. Except for leaving Rafe behind, the kidnappers had been thorough. But why hadn't they slit Rafe's throat? Don't get me wrong, I was glad they hadn't, but why leave a witness? I was going to walk back to where I left him and ask him what he thought about the witness thing, but I didn't have to. He was standing next to the spring watching me.

His skin had gone as pale as the bandage around his head.

"Not a pretty sight," I said.

"What were you doing to them?"

"Seeing if they had any weapons." I rinsed my hands off in the spring.

"And?"

"Nothing." I stood. "Do you remember anything else about the kidnappers?"

He turned away from the bodies. "Not really. I mean, they were dressed like Elham and Ebadullah. Afghans. That's why I thought Ebadullah and Elham were involved."

"After your fall, how long were you out?"

"I don't know. It could have been two minutes or two hours. What difference does it make?"

"Just trying to get an idea of what happened. What did the man squatting over you look like?"

"I already told you. He was an Afghan. A local. Probably Taliban. What are you trying to get at, mate?"

"I'm not sure," I admitted. "I'm just trying to get a clearer picture."

"Where were you?" Rafe asked. "Why didn't you rappel down?"

I'd been waiting for this. "I was asleep. My radio was off."

Rafe laughed, then shrieked in pain. "Ouch!"

Served him right.

"You slept through a kidnapping?" he said. "Oh, that's rich, mate." He started laughing again, this time ignoring the pain.

I hoped his lip started bleeding again. It didn't. I could just imagine him telling everyone he knew how Peak Marcello slept through an abduction.

"Are you done?" I asked.

Rafe stopped laughing, but he was still smiling. At least I think he was smiling. It was hard to tell with his deformed lip. I was tempted to give him my mirror, which would certainly have made the smile go away.

"They didn't know how many climbers were here," I said.

"What do you mean?" Rafe asked.

"I didn't have my tent set up. I don't think they knew I was there."

"Or they knew you were there, and you could have gotten your mum killed by sleeping through the entire thing."

That was one way of looking at it. Another way of looking at it was that they weren't as organized as I had thought. They had no doubt been watching us, but not closely, or they would have known they were missing a climber. Or else it was a targeted kidnapping, meaning they were only interested in one of us, which had to be Alessia, because she was the French ambassador's daughter. This would explain why they didn't kill Rafe when they realized that his injuries would slow them down. I explained my theories to Rafe. When I finished, he offered a theory of his own.

"Plank," he said.

"What?"

"Richest bloke in the world. His climb. His climbers. Ransom. And he'll pay it. He'll have no choice. So there's no point in us running after them. When they get paid, they'll let everybody go. They let me go. Tomorrow we'll head back to the river and wait this out. As long as we don't muck things up, everyone will be perfectly safe."

I turned and shined my headlamp on Elham and Ebadullah. "Not them."

"Collateral damage, mate. They weren't about to take two professional security people with them on a walkabout. Too risky."

"You say the guy squatting over you was Afghan?"

"That's right."

"What did he look like?"

"No idea. He was wearing something over his face. So were the guys standing at the base of the cliff, for obvious reasons. They don't want anyone to ID them after they get their scratch from Plank."

I'd gotten about as much as I was going to get out of Rafe.

"I'm not waiting for tomorrow morning," I said. "I'm heading out now."

"Heading out where?"

I thought back to when Zopa was telling me how to track people across the loose scree, which seemed ridiculous at the time. He obviously didn't know about the abduction then, or he wouldn't have let it happen, but he must have had a premonition that tracking would be important.

"Well?" Rafe said.

"I'm going to try to find them," I said. "You're welcome to head back to the river tomorrow."

"So you're going to leave an injured climber behind?" Rafe said.

"No. I'm just telling you I'm not waiting until tomorrow. I'm leaving now. We should be able to get to the river by first light. I'll leave you there, then continue looking."

"I'm in no condition to stumble over the scree in the dark."

He was probably right, although he hadn't seemed to have any problem finding me in the dark by the spring without a headlamp.

"Where's your headlamp?" I asked.

"Don't know. It must have fallen off when I fell."

"And where's your pack?"

"At the base of the cliff, I guess."

"They asked you to bring your packs?"

"Yeah. Why?"

"No reason." Although it was another piece of the puzzle, which he hadn't mentioned before. "If you want to come with me, let's get your pack and go."

"I already told you I can't make it across the scree in the dark. And going after armed kidnappers is mad. They'll kill you."

It was mad, but if I got caught, I doubted they'd kill me. They hadn't killed Rafe. I would rather have been with Mom and the others than camped at the river worrying about them.

"I'll take you back to base camp," I said. "But we're going now. What you do when you get to the river is up to you. Have you ever ridden a camel?"

"Now what are you talking about?"

INTO THE DARK

IT TOOK RAFE and me a while to find his backpack. It had been ransacked like the other packs, but most of the gear was nearby, including his headlamp. We repacked it, then found the camel munching on some bushes. The next problem was figuring out how to put the saddle on the beast.

"Not a problem," Rafe said. "We have wild camels all over the outback. When I was a kid, I spent my summers leading camel tours around Ayers Rock, or as the aboriginals call it, Uluru."

I knew that Ayers Rock was called Uluru, but I didn't know there were wild camels in Australia.

"Camels are an invasive species, mate," he continued. "The explorers Burke and Wills brought them over for their walkabout in the Never Never. After the car was invented, the camels were set loose. They're a nuisance now, like roos. They shoot camels to control the herds."

He might have been exaggerating about leading the tours, but he certainly seemed to know a lot about camels. He made the camel lie down, or cush, as he called it, which made it relatively easy to get the saddle on. When he got the camel back up, he buckled the saddle on like he'd done it a thousand times before.

"Small camel," he said. "Female. Not big enough for

both of us, but I can haul your pack and the other gear up with me."

There was no debate about who was going to ride the camel, but I didn't mind. I had no desire to ride a camel. He made the camel cush again, then clambered onto the saddle. I handed the gear up, and we headed off into the dark with the donkey trailing behind.

It was a lot easier negotiating the scree without a heavy pack. I kept my head down, looking for the others' trail, but the scree was undisturbed and seemingly endless in my lamplight. I hadn't even picked out the trail we had made getting to the cliff. I had just about resigned myself to hanging in limbo next to the river with Rafe, Ethan, and Cindy—providing Ethan and Cindy hadn't been snatched as well—when my headlamp caught a tiny flash of something white to my left. I stopped and tried to find it again, but the camel bumped into my back, sending me sprawling face first onto the rocks.

"What the bloody . . ."

The rest of Rafe's startled shout was drowned out by the camel bellowing and the donkey braying. I paid no attention to any of it because my fall had reopened the eagle wound on my chin, and I felt warm blood running down my neck. I started swearing too, probably saying worse things than Rafe was shouting, until I realized we were making enough noise to be heard all the way down to the river.

"Quiet!" I shouted.

Apparently both man and beast understood. The cursing, bellowing, and braying stopped immediately, as if I'd punched a mute button. I switched my headlamp off and whispered to Rafe to do the same. Without a word, he complied, and we were wrapped in blackness. It took a while for my eyes to adjust.

"What do you see?" Rafe whispered.

What I expected to see were lights coming our way. No lights. I pushed on my bandage to stem the flow of blood while I scanned the darkness.

"Why did you stop?" Rafe whispered.

I'd almost forgotten why I had stopped. There would be time to look for the white splotch after I figured out if they had heard us or not. "Can you hand down my first aid kit? Don't turn your headlamp on."

"Why?"

"Because it will act like a beacon for the bad guys."

"I get that, mate. Why do you need the first aid kit?"

"Because my face is bleeding."

"Hang on."

I continued to stare into the darkness as he rummaged around behind me, relieved to see there were still no lights.

"What time would you say they took off with the others?" I asked.

"I don't know. Probably around eight."

I looked at my watch. They could have reached the river by now if they had hurried. The darkness would have slowed them up, and so would the hostages. It's not easy to walk with your hands tied behind . . .

"Were their hands tied in front or behind them?"

"What difference does that make?"

It would make all the difference in the world if you were walking downhill over scree. "Humor me," I said.

"In front, I think. Ah, found it."

I walked over and grabbed the kit, but I waited a couple more minutes before using it to make sure there were no lights coming our way.

"I guess we're okay."

"Good. I need to get off and stretch my legs." Rafe made the camel cush and climbed off. "It's uncomfortable."

"When we get going again, do you want to switch?"

"It's not that uncomfortable, and you don't know how to control a camel. It's not as easy as you think."

What I thought was, *If Rafe could do it, a chimp could do it.* What I said was, "I'm sure you're right. I'm going to squat down behind the camel and work on my busted chin with my headlamp on. Keep an eye downhill. If you see a light, let me know."

Rafe said something to the camel and jerked on its halter. The camel bellowed once, then was silent.

"She'll stay down. She's pretty well trained, actually. I'll keep an eye out."

"When I'm done, I'll take a look at your bandages."

I leaned against the camel's warm rump and got the first aid supplies out. The gash on my chin had split open again, but it wasn't nearly as bad as I thought. I cleaned it, put new butterflies on, then rebandaged it.

"Hey, mate! I thought you said you didn't have a mirror."

Crap.

"I thought you were supposed to be looking downhill for lights."

"It's dark as an opal mine. What about the mirror?"

"Didn't know I had one," I lied. "It was at the bottom of the kit."

"Let me see it."

"Sit down and let me look at your bandages first," I said. We switched places. He sat down next to the camel.

"Give me the mirror."

"I wouldn't recommend it."

"You told me it wasn't bad."

"I kind of exaggerated. The good news is that it's a long way from the heart. It'll heal."

Rafe put his hand out. "The mirror, mate."

I gave it to him.

"Good God! I look like the bloody Frankenstein monster!"

Actually he looked worse. "It's not that bad. The swelling has already gone down."

He reached for the bandage around his forehead.

"Don't touch it," I said. "The butterflies are holding it together nicely."

"How long is the cut?"

I cut my answer in half. "A couple inches. We better get going. I'll check the bandages when we get to base camp."

"My lip," Rafe said.

"Yeah, you bit through it, but it's better than it was." It was still pretty hideous, but the swelling *had* gone down some.

"Bloody hell! My earlobe is gone."

There was nothing I could say about the missing earlobe, because the earlobe was gone, and nothing was going to make it better. I stood. I wanted to see if I could spot the white thing that had caused this whole mess. Rafe didn't say a word as I walked away. Too busy wondering what he was going to look like when he healed, I guess.

I stood where I had gotten knocked down, which was pretty easy to find because the scree was disturbed and sprinkled with camel drool and my blood. It took me a while, but I found the white thing about forty feet to my left. It turned out to be a cigarette butt, smoked about halfway down. I examined it closely. Near the filter was the word *Gauloises*. I'd never heard of the brand. I doubted anyone in our group smoked, although Phillip might have been a smoker.

"What are you doing?" Rafe shouted.

"Looking at a cigarette butt," I answered.

"What?"

"Never mind." I didn't want to carry on a shouting conversation across the scree. "We better get moving."

I squatted down, looked across the scree, and smiled, which hurt my chin. It was just like Zopa had explained the night before . . . *This one. And this one. Both turned over earlier today by someone.* But here there were dozens of flipped rocks, making the path as clear as the yellow brick road. Someone was smoking, and someone was dragging his feet. The foot dragger had to be Zopa, and maybe the others too if he had been able to suggest it to them. I started following the path. It was heading down to the river, roughly along a line parallel to the route Rafe and I had been traveling before the camel crash. It wasn't long before Rafe caught up to me on the loping camel with the trailing donkey. He slowed down when he reached me.

"What's with the different route?"

"It's not that much different. Do you see the overturned rocks in front of us?"

"No."

"Probably hard to see from up where you are, but someone is kicking over rocks for us to follow."

"I'm not following anyone. I'm heading back to base camp."

"I get that," I said, a little irritated, although I was happy he was no longer worrying about his ruined face. "We're on our way to the river, which will take us to base camp. One possibility is that they're heading to our base camp as well. In fact, they might already be there, in which case, there won't be a base camp by the time we get there."

This seemed to hit home, because Rafe didn't say a word for the next two miles. Zopa, or whoever was dragging their feet, continued to flip rocks, and I found three more Gauloises cigarette butts. About a mile from the river, their path took a sharp left. It was starting to get light out, which was making the path a little harder to see because there was less contrast. I stopped to reorient myself and get a drink of water.

"Why are you stopping now?" Rafe asked wearily. "We're almost there."

"The path hooks to the northeast here."

"Good. That means they aren't going to base camp." He

pointed to the southwest. "Base camp is that way. We're in the clear."

I was torn. I wanted to dump Rafe and continue following the others, but I had promised that I'd get him back to base camp. Not that he could miss it now. All he had to do was head downhill and, depending where he hit the river, take a right or left.

"How are you feeling?" I asked.

"It's all I can do to keep myself from passing out, mate. My head is exploding. I think I might be having some kind of brain hemorrhage."

I suspected that his brain had been hemorrhaging from the day he was born, but on the off chance that he was having a problem, I was going to have to get him back to base camp.

"Let's go."

I headed southwest, telling myself that it was just as well. I needed to check on Ethan and Cindy, repack my gear, and replenish my water supply. I hadn't had the heart to do it at the spring where Elham and Ebadullah lay.

An hour and a half later, the camp came into view. I stopped to take everything in before we approached.

"Do we have a pair of binoculars?" I asked.

Rafe rummaged around for a minute, then handed a pair down. It was fully light now. There were two tents set up, forty or fifty feet away from each other. A campfire was smoking outside Cindy's tent. The flaps on both tents were closed. I scanned the river. There was no sign of anyone along the shore.

"Well?" Rafe asked.

"Looks like we caught them sleeping."

"Let's wake them up." Rafe slammed his heels into the camel's sides. The camel let out a loud bellow and galloped down to the camp with the braying donkey close behind.

The camel bypassed the tents, running directly down to the river with Rafe shouting, "Whoa! Whoa! Whoa! Stop, you bloody—"

The camel did stop . . . abruptly, at the river's edge, sending Rafe flying into the water. He stood up, drenched and cursing. The camel and donkey drank from the river as if he wasn't there.

SPLIT

Ethan opens his tent flap and steps out into the morning sun scratching his unruly brown hair. I join him.

"What happened to Rafe?"

"He fell off a cliff."

"Land on his head?"

"More or less."

"No harm, then."

I laugh in spite of the circumstances.

"I didn't expect you guys back until this afternoon or evening." He turns and looks up the hill. "Where is everybody?"

"They've been kidnapped."

ETHAN NEARLY FELL, whipping back around to face me. I quickly explained what had happened, leaving out several things like the eagle attack, Zopa's premonition, and Rafe being a jerk, which Ethan probably already knew after spending three minutes with him the day before. Halfway through the summary, a disheveled and exhausted-looking Cindy showed up, and I had to restart the explanation, but only got to *kidnapped* before she started screaming. I should have headed back uphill as soon as Rafe got dunked in the river.

"Are they all right? Where are they? What do the kidnappers want? How did you get away? Are the phones working?"

I didn't have the answers to any of her questions, except how I got away, but I didn't want to get into the I-fell-asleep thing.

"Rafe will fill you in," I said, pointing. He was trudging up from the river, drenched. His head bandage was hanging on his shoulder now, but the butterfly bandages were still holding the gash closed.

"Oh my God!" Cindy shrieked.

"It's not that bad, is it?" Rafe asked, looking as horrified as she did.

"I'm going to get some water, pack some food, and take off," I said. "I found their trail above. I'm going to follow it."

"Which is really stupid," Rafe said. "We need to stick right here so we can be rescued."

"The helicopter won't be here for eight days," Ethan said. "And without a cell or sat signal, we have no way of telling anyone what happened."

"I'm sure the kidnappers have a way of getting their demands out," Rafe said. "Be pretty stupid to nab a bunch of people with no way to let anybody know about it."

"Maybe," Ethan said. "But, rather than sticking in camp, it seems like our best bet would be to head downriver to the nearest village or town. If we get lucky, we might even get a sat or cell signal."

"I wouldn't bet on finding a signal, mate. And the nearest village, if you even want to call it that, is a three- or four-day hike."

"Not in a kayak," Ethan said.

"You have a kayak?"

"Two-person inflatable. Do you know how to use a two-person?"

"Of course I do," Rafe scoffed.

I didn't say anything. Rafe had surprised me with the camel. And the camel surprised him when it saw the river. He very well may have been an expert kayaker. But none of this made any difference to me. I wasn't going with them.

"The water's not that fast here," Ethan said. "But there might be some tricky places downriver were it narrows. If you see trouble ahead, you can always haul out and portage around it. The kayak is as light as a feather."

Cindy's eyes narrowed. "What do you mean by 'you'?"

"I mean you and Rafe. It's a two-person kayak. You two need to get out of here. Get help. Let people know what happened. I'm going with Peak."

This was news to me, but I was happy to hear it.

"What about your ankle?" Cindy asked.

"It's a lot better today than it was yesterday. And it'll be even better tomorrow. I'll use the camel."

"Do you know how to drive a camel?" Rafe asked.

"No, but I've driven a yak, elephant, horse, and car, and flown an airplane. I should be able to figure it out."

"And a snowboard down McKinley," Rafe said with a smirk.

"That's right, mate," Ethan said, returning the smile, then turned to me. "That's if you want me with you."

"Of course," I nearly shouted.

Ethan slapped his hands together. "Great! Then we have a plan."

"No one asked me what I thought," Cindy said.

"Sorry," Ethan said. "If you have a better idea, I'm all ears."

"Two could ride the kayak, and two of us could walk downriver."

I was about to say something, but Ethan beat me to it.

"Except Peak isn't going downriver. He wants to find his mom and the others. And I don't blame him. We can't leave them out there hoping that the kidnappers let them go."

"What are you going to do if you find them?" Cindy asked.

"Exactly," Rafe said. "I asked Peak the same question last night."

"And I bet Peak said that he didn't know," Ethan said.

"That's right," Rafe answered.

"You know," I said, "I'm standing right here."

Ethan laughed. "Sorry. We'll figure it out when we catch up to them—if we catch up to them. It's no different from climbing a mountain that you haven't been up before. You figure it out as you go along. I'm not letting Peak go alone, and if he wasn't going, I might go after them myself."

"Enough of this," I said. "We're wasting time. I'm outta here." I started down to the river to retrieve my gear from the camel.

"Hold on," Ethan said.

I turned my head but kept walking. "What?"

"I'll take care of the gear, drinking water, and kayak.

Why don't you tape Rafe up again? I think I saw some waterproof bandages in Phillip's first aid kit. By the time you get him rewrapped, I'll be ready to go."

Which would probably be another forty-five minutes to an hour—and this was the problem of climbing with other people. I was grateful Ethan wanted to go with me, but I didn't want to wait a second longer. I wanted to find Mom and Zopa and, to be honest, Alessia. And thinking about this brought on a memory that made me smile, unlikely as that was under the horrible circumstances. Mom was not much of a cook. We ate out, or ordered in, almost every night of the week, and it drove me nuts. Not the food, but the *What do you want to eat? Where do you want to eat?* Five different answers every night. My answer was always *I don't care.* It took us longer to decide than it did to get the food and eat it. The memory made me grin.

"What are you grinning at?" Rafe asked, irritably.

"Family dinners," I said, my grin broadening.

SHIP OF THE DESERT

AN HOUR AND FOURTEEN MINUTES later, the ticked-off Cindy and wounded Rafe pushed away from shore and started downriver. They did four complete three-sixties before getting the kayak bow pointed in the right direction. Rafe shouted instructions at Cindy through each revolution, but it seemed to me that it wasn't Cindy causing the problem. It was Rafe.

Ethan shook his head as we watched them disappear around the bend. "I hope they're strong swimmers."

We walked up to where he had tied the camel. Ethan was favoring his right ankle, but not nearly as badly as he had been the day before. The camel looked like she was carrying the entire contents of a flea market on her back.

"I know what you're thinking," Ethan said. "Don't worry. We can get rid of this stuff along the way if we think we can do without it."

"Where are you going to sit?"

"I'm not sure I want to sit up there at all, but I guess I should try so I don't aggravate my ankle, which should be as good as new by tomorrow. What's our next step?"

"I recalibrated my altimeter next to the river. When we get up to where they split off, we'll compare Phillip's drone photos to the topography maps and maybe figure out where they're headed."

"Sounds good to me," Ethan said. "But at some point, you're going to have to get some sleep. You've been up all night stumbling across the scree. You look hammered."

He didn't have to tell me. I felt hammered, but hoped part of it had to do with worry and not exhaustion.

"Let's go," I said.

WE ARRIVED A LITTLE AFTER NOON at the spot where our path had diverged. The scree felt like lava. I stared down at my boots to make sure they weren't on fire. There wasn't a shadow on the entire slope.

I looked up at Ethan. Somehow he had completely changed his appearance. Or else Lawrence of Arabia was on the camel. He was decked out in baggy white cotton pants, a white kurta, and a white keffiyeh on his head, all of which he had managed to change into on camelback without me seeing him.

"You brought that with you?"

Ethan shook his turbaned head. "It's either Elham's or Ebadullah's." He tapped the camel on a front shoulder with a trekking pole. The camel immediately lay down. He climbed off. The donkey trotted over and rubbed against the camel's side.

"Dead man's clothes," I said.

"I don't think they'd mind." Ethan took a long drink of water. "There's a reason they've dressed this way for centuries. My core temp has dropped by at least twenty degrees since I put these on. There's another set if you want them."

"No, I'm good," I said, although I wasn't. I was burning up. I looked at my watch, which my dad had given to me on Everest. It did everything but make him a good dad. It was a hundred and fourteen degrees out. Ten degrees hotter than the day before. It was going to be a long day.

Before Rafe and I headed down to the river, I'd stacked a few rocks up to mark where the trail split. I spread the topo maps and drone photos out on the ground along with the watch that did everything. Plank of course had provided another fancy watch with the gear, but I hadn't taken it out of the box because I hadn't had the time to figure how to use it, what with people getting injured, murdered, and kidnapped.

"So this is where they took off," Ethan said.

I pointed. "To the northeast."

He shaded his eyes and looked in that direction. "Odd, isn't it? It would have been a lot easier for them to head down to the river and follow it east."

"Unless they know something about what lies upriver that we don't know."

"What lies in the direction they're traveling is China."

"I'm sure there's something before China."

"My point is, are you sure this is the way they're headed?"

I looked northeast along the scree. It looked exactly like the scree in every other direction. Undisturbed. What looked like a freeway in the dark looked like a hillside of treacherous rocks the size of fists. If I were in Ethan's boots, I'd be raising the same doubt.

"It was clearer last night when the rocks were freshly flipped. The sun has obviously dried them out. I don't know what else to do but follow along where I think they were headed and hope we stumble across a cigarette butt."

Ethan grinned. "Sounds like a plan. Just checking."

I looked back down at the maps. "I just need to pinpoint where I think we are on the map and photos. I'm hoping to discover something up ahead that—"

"Whoa!"

I looked up, thinking that maybe he had twisted his ankle again. But he was standing right where he had been, staring at his wrist. "GPS," he said.

"What?"

"I have a signal."

I looked at my own watch, and sure enough, the GPS had connected to a satellite a couple hundred miles above us. I now knew exactly where we were, but if we couldn't tell anyone what had happened, it did us little good.

Ethan fished his cell phone out of his pack, turned it on, and shook his head. "No cell towers around here, and Cindy has the only sat phone, which she's probably drowned by now."

"If I'd known, I would have asked her to give it to us," I said.

"And she would have said no way. She found it in Phillip's stuff when her cell went dead. Girl's addicted to her cell. She only has one useful hand. The other hand always has a phone in it."

"I wondered if you and her were—"

Ethan laughed. "Not my type, and I'm not her type either. She was doing that stuff with me at the river to get under Phillip's skin and because she didn't want to go for a hike. The moment you disappeared up the hill, she disappeared into her tent. The only time she came out was to hold a phone above her head to see if she could catch a signal."

I didn't know why, but I was kind of relieved. It wasn't like I cared about who liked whom, but I'd been a little disappointed when it looked like Ethan was interested in Cindy. And I wasn't knocking Cindy. She wasn't the outdoorsy type, and there was nothing the matter with—

What am I doing? I never think like this, and even if I did think like this, now is not the time! What's the matter with me?

I looked at the GPS coordinates on my watch, then tried to find them on the map. For some reason, I was having a hard time with this simple task. The map didn't seem to make any sense to me. Then I forgot the coordinates and had to look at my watch again, and the numbers didn't make sense.

"You're not sweating," Ethan said.

"What?" I looked up and wondered who the man in white was.

The man in white squatted down next to me. "Drink some water."

"Not thirsty."

"You're slurring your words."

"I'm what?"

"Drink. You have heat stroke. I think we need to—"

THE NEXT THING I REMEMBER was a bouncing, rocking sensation. I thought I was in the hull of a ship with my hands and feet tied. My eyes felt like they had been glued shut. I had to rub them to get them open. I was assaulted by a piercing white light. I looked down at my hands. They were tied with climbing rope. There was a climbing harness around my waist cinched down to a . . .

"What is this?" I yelled. "Who—"

The ship came to a sudden stop. I felt myself sinking. The white light disappeared and was replaced by blue sky and Ethan's worried face.

"You okay?"

"Why did you tie me up?" I shouted.

"You're sweating," he said. "That's great."

"So you were with them from the very beginning!" I jerked on the ropes.

Ethan's expression changed from worry to utter confusion. "What are you talking about?"

"You're with them!" I shouted.

My outraged accusation did not cause the reaction I thought it would. Ethan started laughing. Which enraged me even more. If my hands hadn't been tied, I would have strangled him.

"Chill out," he said. "You'll hurt yourself. I'll untie you."

This stalled my outrage. I began to think that maybe I had misjudged the situation. Ethan was being too reasonable and cheerful. I stopped struggling, but I continued to glare at him as he loosened the ropes.

"Sorry about the tie job," he said. "But I didn't know any other way to keep you on the camel after you conked out."

"Conked out?"

"Yeah. Eyeballs rolled up to the top of your sockets. Caught you before you did a face plant on the rocks. For a second, I thought I'd lost you to the great beyond. Managed to get you cooled off and hydrated. Had to get you out of your clothes into something cooler."

I looked down at what I was wearing. Baggy cotton pants and a kurta. Dead man's clothes, which I have to say were more comfortable than climbing pants and a T-shirt.

"I wet you down and rigged a shelter with tent poles on the back of the camel," he continued. "The problem was keeping you in place. Had to truss you up to keep you from falling off and cracking your head on the rocks."

It started to come back to me. Not the kurta, the wetting, or the trussing, but the reason he had to tend to me.

"Heat stroke," I said.

"Bigtime. More like heat fist. A knockout."

Ethan got the last knot undone. I rubbed my numb wrists.

"So you're not a terrorist or a kidnapper."

"Sorry to disappoint," Ethan said with a grin. "Just a common climber. Heat stroke is bad news. I had it once. Not as bad as your dose, but bad enough. It was disorienting. When I snapped out of it, I had no idea what had happened. Didn't know where I was for a while. I got it the same way you did. Exhausted, stressed, dehydrated . . . pushed my body too hard, and my body pushed me over the edge." He handed me a bottle of water.

I took a sip. "Where are we?"

"Still heading northeast."

"How long was I out?"

Ethan looked at his watch. "A little over four hours."

I clambered off the camel on shaky legs. Ethan grabbed my arm to steady me. We were still on scree, but the rocks were bigger than the rocks we'd been traversing earlier. To the north of us was a towering hill covered in trees, shrubs, and boulders the size of cars.

Ethan handed me a white cotton cloth the size of a pillowcase.

"Make yourself a keffiyeh like mine," he said. "No arguments. Secure it with your headlamp. You gotta keep the sun off."

I draped it over my head and immediately felt cooler. Ethan pulled my headlamp out of my pack. I slipped it over the cloth, certain I looked as ridiculous as he did, but I didn't care. It was perfect for the conditions. If I'd had it on earlier, I might not have *conked out,* as he put it.

I pointed. "What's on the other side of the hill?"

Ethan grinned. "A valley."

"Very funny. All hills have valleys. I'm serious. Did you look at the map?"

"Yeah. There's a valley and, beyond that, a plateau. When you checked out on me, I thought about taking you back to the river, but that wouldn't have gotten us any closer to the perps. With nine captives, they have to be heading someplace that has food, water, and shelter, and it has to be close, because they're on foot. My guess is they're hiding out in the valley."

"How's your ankle?"

"Not bad. I wrapped it, and I've been using the trekking poles."

"Sorry I passed out. If you hadn't—"

"No problem," Ethan interrupted. "You're still going to have to take it easy. Heat stroke can kill you."

"Well, thanks for taking care of me."

I should have thanked him for *saving* me. If Ethan hadn't been there, I might have died on the blistering scree. I looked up at the hill again.

"Looks pretty lush compared to the scree."

Ethan followed my gaze. "Definitely water on the other side. A stream or two running down to the river. And we need water. I used all but a pint putting out your heat stroke."

"Are you sure they came this way?"

Ethan reached into his pocket and pulled out a handful of cigarette butts. "Hansel and Gretel have a bad nicotine habit. Gauloises and Marlboros. Unless one of them is smoking two different brands, at least two of them are smokers."

I looked at my watch. We had about five hours of daylight left. Plenty of time to reach the valley on the other side of the steep hill. The GPS was still working. "Let's look at the map."

The valley had a blue river or stream line snaking down the center of it. I followed the blue with my finger. By the elevation markings, it looked like it ran through a deep gorge and emptied into the river where our base camp had been.

"Looks pretty rugged," Ethan said.

"Which is why they didn't take the easy path along the river."

Ethan nodded. "Which means they know a lot more about this terrain than we do."

"They have to be locals," I said.

Ethan shook his head. "Maybe one or two of them. I've been thinking about that. Aside from Plank, the only people who knew where we were climbing were Phillip and Zopa, and I don't think they told anybody."

"How about the helicopter pilot?"

"Maybe. But I didn't get the kidnapper-terrorist vibe from him. Did you?"

"To be honest, I didn't pay much attention to him at all," I admitted. "The only impression I got was that he was in a hurry to dump us and get back to Kabul." I folded the map. "We better get moving if we want to get to the first valley before dark."

Ethan shaded his eyes and looked at the hill.

"A bit of a hike," he said.

THE HIKE

It's more than a bit of a hike. The first thing we discover is that kurtas and baggy pants are not designed for clambering up incredibly steep hills, sometimes on all fours. They tear easily and get tangled. We change back into our pants but keep the keffiyehs on our heads. The second thing we discover is that camels are not designed for steep rocky inclines. A third of the way up, our camel balks, becoming as immovable as the boulders we are winding our way around. No amount of shouting, tugging, or prodding will make her take another step. The donkey becomes so incensed by our efforts, it bites Ethan in the butt . . .

"OUCH!"

"Now you can say you've been bitten in the ass by an ass."

"That's not funny," Ethan said, rubbing his gluteus maximus.

"Yeah, it is. What do you want to do?"

"Cut this cantankerous camel loose."

We unloaded everything, took off the saddle and halter, and sorted through the gear. I suggested we take only what we needed.

"You never know what you'll need," he said. "I think I'll take everything I own."

I dumped half my stuff to make room for extra climbing gear.

During all of this, the camel didn't move and was still glued in place as we put on our packs and continued up the hill. I looked back after a few yards and was happy to see that she and the donkey were slowly making their way back down the hill.

Carrying the packs made the climb more difficult, but on the bright side, it was cooler with the trees and shrubs, maybe 100 degrees instead of 110 degrees, and we were on the right track. Every few feet, we spotted a perfectly clear footprint in the dust, almost as if someone was leaving it there for us to follow.

"Zopa," I said.

"How do you know? It could be anyone's. Do you know Zopa's boot pattern?"

"No, but I know Zopa's personality pattern, and I bet you a dollar this is his boot."

"You're on. Of course, I won't be able to collect if we don't find water on the other side of this hill."

With that grim thought, we continued on. Halfway up the hill, we stopped and shared the last pint of water, which did nothing to slake our thirst. Ethan was right. If we didn't find water on the other side, there was a good chance we wouldn't be leaving Afghanistan alive.

Two-thirds of the way up, my prediction that we would reach the valley on the other side before dark was shattered. The sun went down.

"At least the moon is full," Ethan said.

The moon was bright, but not bright enough to light our way. We would have to use our headlamps.

Ethan sat down on a boulder. "I don't know about you," he said, "but I'm bushed."

I was too, and he was carrying at least twenty more pounds than I was. I joined him on the boulder. We sat there for several minutes, catching our breath.

"I'm tempted to camp right here," Ethan said.

"How's your ankle?"

"I can barely feel it among my other aches."

"It'll be cooler with the sun down."

"I'm not serious about staying here," Ethan said. "We have to find water. I just need to rest for a bit."

I needed to sleep for a week.

"I don't think I thanked you for coming along with me," I said.

"Forget it."

"Why did you come?" I knew why I was following them. My mom, Zopa, and now Alessia. I had a feeling that Zopa wanted me to follow him. That somehow he knew I would follow. But why had Ethan come? He barely knew any of us, including the film crew.

"To be honest, I don't know," he answered. "And to be even more honest, I've been having second thoughts with each step I've taken up this miserable hill, which I think we should start calling a mountain, because that's what it feels like to me. But getting back to your question, I guess I tagged along because it seemed like the right thing to do. Call it a sense of duty. My alternatives were to stay at camp, head downstream with Rafe and Cindy, or go after the bad guys with you. The bad guys won out. Most people run away from bad guys. It's kind of fun running toward them."

"You know I don't have a plan," I said. "I mean, other than to catch up with them."

Ethan grinned. "You mean we're not going to bust in on them like a couple of action heroes, take the dirtbags out, and free the hostages?"

I laughed. "Nah. What's probably going to happen is that we're going to become hostages ourselves."

"We'll see." Ethan stood up and stretched. "Remind me to tell you what I did for a living before I became an adrenaline-addicted climbing junkie."

"Why don't you tell me now?"

"Because we have to top this mountain and find water before we die."

WE TOPPED THE HILL, which did feel like a mountain, a little before midnight. After a brief discussion about staying where we were until morning, we started down the other side, which in a way was worse than going up because we had to spend most of it sliding on our butts. Midway down, Ethan found a crumpled cigarette package. *Gauloises.*

"French brand," Ethan said, reading the package.

"I don't think Alessia smokes."

"Yeah, but it's interesting that someone smokes French cigarettes. I'm not sure how easy French cigarettes are to get in Afghanistan."

"Rafe said they were Afghans."

"You look like an Afghan with that keffiyeh."

I'd forgotten that I was wearing it. "Are you saying they're French?"

"Nope. I'm saying we have no idea who these guys are, or what they want, and we need to keep our minds open."

"So, what did you do before you were an adrenaline-addicted climbing junkie?"

"I was an MP."

"Member of Parliament?"

Ethan laughed. "Just as unlikely. Military policeman. Marine Corps."

"No way!"

"Six years." He saluted. "Got into a little jam when I was seventeen. It was either serve time in the military or serve time in jail. I chose to join the marines."

I had gotten into a little jam myself earlier in the year. It was either leave the country for a while or be locked in juvenile detention until I was eighteen.

"Your nickname," I said.

Ethan nodded. "Yep, I was a sergeant."

"Were you in Afghanistan?"

Ethan shook his head. "I was in Iraq a couple of times, but only briefly. I worked mostly stateside."

"Doing what?"

"Busting military criminals and killers trained by the U.S. government. It was interesting work."

"Why did you leave?"

"I wasn't exactly a model soldier. I was terrible at following orders and keeping my mouth shut when something needed to be said. Despite this, they would have kept me on because I was a pretty effective cop, but I opted out.

There were mountains to climb. To make money, I work for a buddy of mine from the corps who hires me as a security consultant."

"What's that?"

"Basically a highly paid bodyguard for government dignitaries and rich people. The money's good, but I don't like the work. That's why I hooked up with JR's crew as a climbing consultant. They're only paying expenses, but I figured that I could learn the documentary business from them. I'm tired of others making money off my exploits. I'd like to do my own documentaries."

"So you know what to do about the kidnappers?"

"I wouldn't go that far," he answered. "But I do have some experience in handling smart killers. What I don't have are weapons, and of course the Marine Corps backing me up. We're at a distinct disadvantage, but it's not totally hopeless."

"Unless we don't find water at the bottom of this hill."

"Right. If we don't find water . . ."

He didn't have to finish the question. We continued our downhill slide.

THEY SAY WATER IS ODORLESS, but I'm not sure this is true. I swear I could smell it from fifty yards away. Ethan could too by the way he half walked, half stumbled toward the source at the bottom of the hill.

We were going to live a while longer. There was a good-size stream, ten feet across, with a good flow. It was the sweetest and coldest water I had ever tasted.

"Take it slow," Ethan warned, but neither of us did.

I must have scooped half a gallon of water into my mouth without ill effect. When I paused to look over at Ethan, he was still scooping water into his mouth as fast as he could.

"We should eat something," I said.

Ethan looked at me through dull, tired eyes. "Yeah, I guess we should."

But we didn't. Somewhere between unzipping my pack and pulling out my camp stove, I fell asleep, passed out, keeled over, or a combination of all three.

THE GHOST CAT

I open my eyes. I can hear the stream bubbling past a few feet away. It's still dark. The full moon shines through the tree branches above me, casting the forest in pale blue light. There's a fine mist in the air. I'm cold, but unable to do anything about it. With great effort, I twist my head toward the stream with a vague feeling that something, or someone, is watching me. I see Ethan lying on his back, his arms spread out above his head, his legs splayed as if he's dead. But he isn't. I can hear him gently snoring. He must have fallen straight back from where he'd been kneeling next to the stream. I catch a flicker of movement just beyond him on the other side of the stream. I squint my eyes, trying to focus in the dark. The movement comes again—a thick, smoke-colored tail. The shen *is crouched down, staring at me. I want to tell Ethan, but my throat doesn't seem to work. The only thing that comes out of my mouth is my breath on the cold air. The tail flicks twice more, then the cat reels around and disappears into the forest without a sound, like a ghost . . .*

I BLINKED AWAKE. The sun was high above the trees. I sat up in a panic and looked at my watch, then looked at it again in disbelief. It was five minutes past noon. I had slept the morning away.

"Afternoon," Ethan said.

He was sitting next to the stream with his feet in the water. Sitting next to him on a flat rock was a camp stove with something steaming inside a pot.

"How could you let me sleep? You should have gotten me up."

"I've only been awake fifteen minutes—or resurrected, because what happened last night felt more like death than sleep."

"We better get packed and moving." I looked at my pack and realized there was nothing to pack because I hadn't unpacked anything.

"Not before we eat something." Ethan tossed me a protein bar. "I'm boiling water for oatmeal and tea. We need to replenish ourselves, or we're no good to anyone."

I knew he was right, but I still wanted to get moving. "We can eat on the way."

"Now's not the time to get antsy," Ethan said. "We've got to move cautiously. They were here, and not that long ago."

"How do you know?"

"Footprints all over the place."

I walked over to the stream. There were a half dozen muddy boot prints heading upstream.

"They could be a hundred yards, or twenty miles, ahead. I know you don't care if we're captured, but I'd prefer we not round a corner and blunder into their backs."

Seeing the footprints reminded me of what I'd seen in the dark, or what I thought I'd seen. I waded across the stream. In the soft mud were four perfectly formed *shen* paw prints.

"What are you looking for?" Ethan asked from across the stream.

"A ghost," I answered.

GRAVE

It doesn't take us long to eat and start upstream. I'm still tired, but it feels good to move. After a mile, my muscles warm and loosen. Ethan, or Sergeant Todd, the most unlikely marine there ever was, is in the lead, setting an easy but steady pace. It's humid next to the stream, with the trees, plants, shrubs, and birds, not at all what I picture when I think of Afghanistan, but I pay little attention to the scenery and the sounds. Instead I focus on the boot prints in the soft mud. Two of the prints are smaller than the others and leave different patterns. Mom's and Alessia's. As long as they are walking, they are okay. It's been nearly forty-eight hours since they were taken . . .

"WHOA!" ETHAN SAID.

I jogged up to where he had stopped. He was pointing at a tangle of muddy boot prints, and in the center of the smallest boot print was a paw print.

"Snow leopard," I said.

"How do you know?"

I told him about seeing the snow leopard at the stream and on the cliff.

"So it's stalking us," Ethan said.

"I don't think snow leopards are dangerous. I think it's just watching us, or maybe watching *over* us."

Ethan grinned. "You're not going all magical thinking on me, are you?"

I returned the grin. "It works for Zopa. And we could use some magic."

"You got that right. Wish I had a magic wand, or an invisibility cloak. But I do think we're getting closer."

"A magical feeling?"

"Nah, the boot prints look fresher, and by the way they lie in the mud, they moved pretty fast through here."

"They teach you that in the marines?"

Ethan nodded. "I spent a couple years in Force Reconnaissance or Force Recon. They're the guys that sneak around behind enemy lines and gather intelligence before the main force makes its push. It was a lot of fun until some gung-ho captain walked us into quicksand, which killed two men. He blamed us and became a major. I switched to the MPs and busted him a year and a half later for stealing guns and selling them on the black market. He's in prison. I'm climbing mountains."

HALF A MILE UPSTREAM, we came to a place where they had obviously stopped for a while. There were food wrappers lying around a couple of dead campfires.

"Let me check this out before we tromp through," Ethan said.

I sat down on a log and watched him, happy for the rest. He crept around, sometimes crouching to look at the ground, sometimes standing and doing a slow three-sixty of the area.

"I'd guess they were here for a couple hours. Their first

long stop, which means they left the cliffs, topped the hill, and walked all the way here until they bedded down to rest. That tells us that the perps are in better shape than we are."

"That can't be good."

"You got that right. And there's worse news. Come over here."

He was standing next to one of the campfires. I joined him.

He pointed at the ground. "See those?"

"Boot prints?" There were a lot of them.

Ethan shook his head. "The three little holes in the mud. Here, here, and here. They were left by a camera tripod. They were filming something. Or mounted the camera to a . . ." Ethan swore.

"What?"

"Maybe you should stay here."

"What are you talking about?"

"The mounds," he said quietly.

There were three of them, made out of rocks, thirty feet away. I ran over to them. The piles were about six feet long and three feet wide.

"Graves," Ethan said. "Maybe we should just leave them be. There's nothing we can do to help them now."

"No," I said.

I dropped down to my knees and started moving rocks. The first grave was Phillip's. Like Elham and Ebadullah, his throat had been slit. I didn't want to uncover the other two, but I had to know. The second was Aki. The third was Choma. I sat back, covered my face, and began sobbing with horror and relief. It could have been Mom or Zopa or Alessia or the film crew. I felt angry, afraid, and guilty. Angry because Phillip, Aki, and Choma didn't deserve to die. Afraid because there might be other graves ahead. Guilty because I was relieved that there was no one I loved among the dead.

By the time I looked up, Ethan had replaced the rocks, but this did nothing to erase the memory. Like mine, his face was streaked in tears, but there was a hard, determined set to his jaw. I think if the kidnappers had showed up right then, he would have tried to tear them apart with his bare hands.

"This changes everything," he said. "You need to head back to base camp the way we came, try to catch up with Cindy and Rafe."

"Forget it," I said.

"You're not trained for this."

"And you are?"

"Not exactly," Ethan admitted. "But the corps did teach me a few things."

"I'm going with you," I said. "Or I'm going on my own. I didn't ask you to come with me."

"I don't think you understand how serious this is."

"I understood how serious it was when I found Elham and Ebadullah murdered during their evening prayer."

Ethan glared. I glared back. Ethan looked away. I'd won. If you call probably getting killed somewhere upstream a victory. I had gone after the other climbers with the assumption that the kidnappers wouldn't harm me because they hadn't hurt the others and had let Rafe go. I was clearly wrong about that, but it didn't change anything.

After seeing the bodies, I was even more determined to get to Mom regardless of the consequences. Apparently, Ethan was thinking along the same lines.

He said, "Okay, then, we're both dead."

"Not necessarily."

"No, absolutely," he insisted. "We are dead men. We died right here. We have no weapons, there are only two of us, and we have no idea what lies ahead or even how many bad guys we're up against. The only way to play this is to get it into your mind right now that you died. That's not to say we're going to play this stupid like a couple of mindless zombies, but the only way to win this, the only chance we have, is to wrap your mind around the fact that you have already died, and you can't die again, because you are already dead. Can you do this?"

Ethan grinned, but it wasn't his normal charming isn't-life-amusing grin. It was kind of a scary I-have-lost-my-mind grin. He pointed down at the foot of the three graves. "It's get-real-brutally-honest time. What do you see?"

I saw three round holes in the shape of a pyramid. "Tripod," I said.

Ethan nodded. "These dirtbags made the video crew film our friends' execution. They're going to use the tape to get money." He pointed at the graves. "These three were expendable, but it could have just as easily been your mom, Zopa, or the film crew. I think everyone is expendable, except for maybe Alessia."

"Why Alessia?"

"Because the U.S. has a long history of not negotiating with terrorists or hostage takers. Not so the French.

Over the years, they've paid out millions of euros in ransom money. My guess is that some of these guys are French, ex-military, and they've probably been targeting Alessia for months."

"How do you know they're French?"

"Gauloises. The only people I have ever seen smoke those nasty things are the French. When I was in Iraq, we broke up a tobacco-smuggling operation. Some of our guys were involved in it. Learned more than I ever wanted to know about tobacco. There are a lot of counterfeit cigarette operations. The Taliban actually make money here running cigarettes when they aren't smuggling dope. Anything for a buck. Some of the Taliban cigarette exports made it over to Iraq. Counterfeit Turkish brands, American brands, Pakistani brands, no French brands. I'm not saying for certain the perps are French, but I'm leaning that way. And as far as them being military or ex-military, I'm judging that by their physical condition. They got a lot farther than we did before they stopped here, and they were herding a large group of hostages. They're probably ex-commandos."

It finally dawned on me what he was getting at. "But we're not afraid of them," I said. "Because the worst they can do is kill us, and we're already dead."

"Now you're talking." Ethan's skeletal grin broadened. He had dropped at least ten pounds since I had met him in New York. I supposed I had lost some weight too.

"Let's get back to the tripod and what happened here," Ethan said. "Somehow these guys got wind of Alessia going on this climb. The corridor is the perfect place to set up the grab. It's no man's land. The reason you got left behind is that they didn't have any idea how many climbers there were. They probably didn't know that Cindy and I were at base camp either. They left Rafe behind because they already had too many people and hoped he would die from his injuries. Lucky for him, because he would have been lying right next to these guys if he hadn't been injured. I think they executed the weak links."

"Aki and Choma were pretty strong," I said. "As strong as the film crew, anyway."

"Yeah, but they didn't know how to use the camera and sound equipment. I suspect Phillip was mouth breathing by the time he got here. And probably mouthing off too. Bottom line, they culled their hostages like they were cattle. I bet they made them dig the shallow graves themselves and had the survivors cover the dead with rocks."

"Why bury them at all?" I asked. "They didn't bury Elham and Ebadullah."

"They were in a hurry when they left the cliff. Totally exposed on the scree until they got to the hill and down into the valley. The reason they buried these guys is because of vultures."

"What?"

"Soaring vultures are a dead giveaway. No pun intended. Which probably means their hideout is somewhere up this valley."

"How did they know where we were going to be?"

"I have no idea. People inside the French embassy had to know where Alessia was going ahead of time. She's the ambassador's kid. Plank had to jump through some bureaucratic hoops to get permission for her to go, which means these guys probably know that the richest man in the world is behind the climb. Two pots of gold at the end of the rainbow. Plank's and the French government's. I think they'll try to dip into both of them. The vid they shot here is their terrible calling card."

THE WALKING DEAD

It's a little hard to wrap my mind around being dead with my legs aching and a heavy pack on my back, but I'm getting there with each step I take upstream. I'm not sure I buy Ethan's theory as to who the perps are, but it doesn't matter. The only thing that matters now is finding them. Ethan is in the lead, moving cautiously. We tightened down the gear on our packs to silence the rattle. We haven't spoken since we left the graves . . .

ETHAN STOPPED NEXT to the stream. Judging by the number of footprints in the mud, the captives had stopped there as well, but there was one set of prints that looked fresher than the others—much fresher. I pointed them out. Ethan squatted down.

"A few hours old," he said quietly. "The other prints are a lot older. Yesterday, I'd say."

"Those newer-looking prints belong to one of the kidnappers," I said.

"How do you know that?"

I'd been paying close attention to the tracks for the last several miles, trying to memorize the patterns and guess which pattern belonged to whom. As long as there were tracks, the others were alive. Mom's and Alessia's were the easiest because their feet were smaller. Mom was wearing hiking boots, because she had been on the ground when they were captured. Alessia was wearing climbing shoes. They hadn't allowed her to change out of them, which could not have been very comfortable. Climbing shoes aren't designed for walking. The film crew was also wearing climbing shoes—identical climbing shoes because the patterns were all the same. Zopa was wearing boots. His tracks were easy to pick out in the soft ground because he walked with his feet splayed out. The other boots on the ground were the bad guys.

I explained my theory to Ethan.

"How many kidnappers are there?" he asked.

"I think there are four."

"Useful information."

"I could be wrong."

"We'll find out soon enough." Ethan pointed at the fresh prints. "Let's see what this guy was up to."

We followed the prints over to the stream. They stopped at a shallow pool. On either side of the prints were several round indentations the size of dinner plates.

"Water containers?" I asked.

"That would be my guess. Four of them. If they were a gallon each, he walked away from here carrying thirty-two pounds of water."

"Which means they're close," I said.

"Absolutely. When you fetch that much water, you don't go a step farther than you have to. This also means that their hideout isn't next to the stream."

"And it's on this side of the stream," I added.

"There are at least ten people. In this heat, sixteen quarts of water aren't going to last long. This could have been his

last water trip of the day, but I doubt it. I think they'll make
another water run before dark. It's kind of a risk, but I say
we conceal ourselves on the other side of this stream and
try to get a look at our enemy before we make our move."

I wanted to follow the boot prints to wherever they were
holding the others, storm the entrance, and save my mom
before they slit her throat.

"Are we still dead?" I asked.

"Of course," Ethan answered. "What's your point?"

"So the guy may, or may not, come down here. We already know he's armed and in great shape. What's to be
gained by getting a glimpse of him? We need to figure out
where they're holding our friends and do something about
it before anyone else gets killed."

"Maybe I'm not quite as dead as I'm letting on," Ethan
said. "Old habits die hard. I was trying to gather intelligence. That may not be a dead-man thing to do, but I think
we're lucky we didn't blunder into the water guy when we
got here. He would have shot or captured us."

"That's it!" I said.

"What's it?"

"Blunder. Capture. Do you have a two-way?"

Ethan nodded.

"Me too. You're after intelligence, right?"

"Yeah, but—"

"When he comes down for water, I'll *blunder* into him
like I'm out looking for the others. I'll let him capture me.
We'll tape down the talk button on the two-way. Have to
figure a way to conceal it so he doesn't find it. You'll hear
everything that's going on. I'll try to feed you information,

or intelligence, about where we're being held, how many people there are, what kind of weapons, what kind of security they have in place."

"Then I come in and save you," Ethan said.

"Something like that. Didn't the Marine Corps teach you how to—"

"Kill people?" Ethan asked.

"Right. Kill people."

"As a matter of fact, they did. In a lot of different ways. But I never had to put any of that training into play, I'm happy to say. And what if you blunder into this guy and he simply shoots you in the head?"

"What difference does it make? I'm already dead."

"All I'm saying is that maybe I should be the guy that does the blundering. If he decides to shoot first, I'd have a better chance of taking him down than you do."

"And if he doesn't shoot you, and you get captured, what then? You could feed me all the information you want, but there is nothing I could do with it. The only thing I know how to do is climb. I'm not a marine."

"Neither am I," Ethan said. "Not anymore. But I get your point. How do you want to play this?"

"I guess I'll go downstream a ways and wait. When I see him, I'll walk up to him."

Ethan shook his head. "If you're set on doing this, you need to do it right. I think it would be better to let him blunder into you rather than you blundering into him. You need to look completely defenseless so he doesn't shoot you on the spot."

"I am completely defenseless," I pointed out.

"Yeah, but he won't know that. I think you should set up camp right here. Roll out your sleeping bag, have something cooking on the camp stove, maybe even pretend like you've dozed off or passed out from exhaustion. These guys are ruthless, but I doubt they'd shoot you while you're sleeping."

Ethan was obviously forgetting that they murdered Elham and Ebadullah while they were praying, but I liked his plan better than mine.

We got the two-ways, put them on the same frequency, taped my transmit button on with duct tape, then spent five minutes debating where we should put my "wire" as Ethan called it. Fortunately the two-way was pretty compact, about the size of a small sponge, although not nearly as soft. We decided to strap it to my side under my arm with an Ace bandage and a sock underneath to stop chafing and soak up the sweat. I put on my baggiest T-shirt and modeled it for Ethan.

"Perfect. Of course, if he frisks you, it's all over."

With that happy thought, Ethan waded across the stream. We tested the wire one more time. He gave me a thumbs-up, then disappeared into the trees.

BLUNDER

I have water heating on the camp stove for oatmeal and raisins. I have my sleeping bag rolled out. The two-way strapped to my side itches. I wonder how long the battery is going to last with the transmit button on. I wonder how long it's going to be before water guy shows, or if he'll show at all. It's getting dark. The water comes to a boil. I pour in my packet of oatmeal. Stir. I hear my mother scream—

I WHIPPED AROUND, sending the camp stove and oatmeal flying. Mom was standing in front of a giant with a gun, pounding on his chest with her bound hands. He pushed her away. She stumbled backwards and fell. He pointed his pistol at her, thumbing the hammer back.

"No!" I shouted.

He pointed the pistol at me.

"No!" Mom shouted, then started pleading with him in French.

The giant appeared to be listening to her, considering, the pistol still pointing at me. He was at least six foot four, three feet across the chest, and two feet at the waist. Muscles were literally bubbling out of the tight camouflaged T-shirt he wore. A lot of times musclebound hulks like him have absolutely zero endurance, but in his case, I knew better. The route they had traveled to get here was brutal, but he looked perfectly fine. Ethan had been right about their condition and nationality. But the thing that really scared me was that his face wasn't covered. I'd be able to pick him out of a thousand photos in an instant. This could only mean that he had no intention of letting me or Mom or anyone else identify him. No one was getting away. They were going to kill us. And I thought he might do it right then.

Mom finished her plea. He looked at her with cool, intelligent gray eyes. His long black hair was pulled back into a ponytail. He wore a brown sweatband around his forehead. He said nothing. Scattered around the ground were a half dozen collapsible plastic water containers. They must have dropped them before I was able to turn around.

He finally said something to Mom. She got on her stomach with her zip-tied hands stretched out above her head.

"He wants you to lie down next to me and assume the same position. Don't try anything. If he even thinks you're making a wrong move, he'll kill us both."

I walked over to her, resisting the urge to raise my hands above my head. If I did, he might see the bulge on my right side. I lay down next to her and put my elbows at my sides with my hands up to keep the two-way covered. He stepped around in back of us. I felt him kick my legs apart, then the search began. Right leg, left leg, butt, pockets . . . if he patted me down above the waist, we were dead. But he didn't. He came back around to the front and said something to Mom.

"*Non*," she said. "He wanted to know if you spoke French."

"Does he speak English?"

"I think he understands a little."

I was going to have to be very careful about what I said. The interrogation began, with Mom translating.

He wanted to know how I got there. I told him that I had fallen asleep in the cave. When I woke up, everyone was gone except for Elham and Ebadullah, who had been murdered, and Rafe, who looked like he had died in a fall. I took off in the dark and got lost, disoriented. My water ran out. I climbed the hill, thinking there might be a stream on the other side, and if there was, I might be able to follow it down to the river. I found a stream and was going to follow it down, but I came across footprints heading upstream and followed them instead.

He wanted to know if I had seen the graves.

I acted like I didn't know what he was talking about.

He wanted to know what I had hoped to accomplish by following them.

I said I wanted to find my mother and the others.

It went on like this for ten more minutes, then the questions abruptly stopped. He looked up at the darkening sky, then back down at us, pistol still cocked and ready. After what seemed like an eternity, he said something to Mom. She nodded.

"We can get up," she said. "He wants to search your pack."

His technique for searching my pack was to have me unzip every pocket and shake the contents out onto the ground. When he finished toeing the gear and clothes with his boots, he stomped on the pack to make sure it was empty. My knife and anything else that might be used as a weapon were kicked into the stream.

"You can repack," Mom said. "Quickly."

The guy talked to her while I stuffed everything back into the pack. I wondered if Ethan spoke French and was picking any of it up. Or was the battery already dead? Was all this for nothing? I finished about the same time he finished talking to Mom. If I got out of this alive, I swore I was going to learn French and several other languages.

"Okay," Mom said. "Here's the deal. He's going to cut me loose because you'll be my new cuffs. If I try anything, he'll kill you. If you try anything, he'll kill me. You shouldn't have followed us."

"I had to."

"They've already killed Phillip, Choma, and Aki."

I tried to look shocked. The guy pulled a knife out, flicked it open, and sliced through the plastic zip-ties around Mom's wrists. I wondered if the knife had been used to slit the others' throats.

Mom rubbed the feeling back into her hands. "This is the first time they've used one of us to haul water."

Which accounted for the fact that her footprints hadn't been with his next to the stream.

We grabbed the containers and started filling them. The French guy stood ten feet behind, the pistol pointed at our backs. With him standing that far back and the stream masking my voice, I thought it was safe to talk if I kept my voice down. I tried an experimental question.

"Does this guy have a name?"

"We don't know his real name so we call him Géant,

French for *giant*," she whispered. "The other Frenchman, who you'll meet if Géant doesn't kill us, we call Émile."

"Ethan is watching and listening to us on the other side of the stream," I said quietly. "I have a two-way strapped to my side."

I wondered if she had heard what I had said. Without a word, she filled her container, screwed on the cap, and grabbed the next one. I did the same.

"We need to feed Ethan as much information as we can," I said.

She gave me a very slight nod. "We are being kept in a cave half a mile away. Three Frenchmen. Three Afghans. Professionals. Weapons. An Afghan and one of the Frenchmen left yesterday to take the ransom video to Kabul. There are four at the cave now. Géant, Émile, two Afghans. When they have their money, they will kill all of us."

Géant stepped closer and said something.

"Hurry," Mom said. "He wants to get back before dark. The others were killed because they were slowing us down."

We hurried.

THE CAVE

Moving up a darkening trail with sixteen pounds of water in each hand, a pack on your back, and a guy with a pistol behind you is hard. What makes it even more difficult is trying to give information to Ethan in code so I don't get shot in the back of the head. My worry is that the two-way won't work inside the cave, or the battery is already gone.

"So everyone's okay?" I ask Mom.

"Yes."

"All in the same place?"

"Yes. A cavern a hundred feet from the entrance to the cave. Straight back. There's an Afghan outside the entrance of the cavern twenty-four-seven."

"One way into the cave?"

"It's like a rabbit warren. I suspect there's more than one way inside, but I don't know where it is."

Géant doesn't seem to mind us talking, but I don't want to push my luck. I stay quiet until we reach the cave . . .

WE STOPPED NEXT to a vertical wall covered in plants and shrubs. I didn't see a cave opening at first. Géant said something, and a rope dropped down from a narrow opening in the tangle.

"Thirty feet up," I said. There was no way the radio was going to transmit from inside the deep cave unless Ethan was directly in front of it. I looked back at the trail we'd just walked. There were some good-size climbable trees that might give him a line of sight to the opening, but how was I going to convey that without Géant figuring out what I was doing?

Mom came to the rescue. "Help me tie the bottles onto the rope," she said. "When they have the water up, they'll throw down a thirty-foot rope ladder. I'm not sure why they're using a ladder. Climbing the wall would be easier than climbing one of the trees across from the cave."

I looked at Géant. He didn't blink at this exchange. He obviously didn't understand what she had just said. I just hoped Ethan did.

We got the bottles tied to the rope, and someone heaved them up.

"Émile is on the other end of the rope," Mom said. "He speaks perfect English. You'll have to watch what you say."

What I was watching was how strong Émile was. The water jugs flew up the side as if they were empty. As soon as they disappeared, a rope ladder was tossed out of the entrance.

"I'll go first to run interference," she said. "You're going to get grilled again."

I followed her up.

Émile was almost as tall as Géant, but leaner, with short blond hair and blue eyes. Like Mom predicted, he asked me roughly the same questions as Géant, but in English. Midway through the grilling, Géant clambered into the cave and pulled the ladder up behind him. When he stood up, he had to stoop so he didn't scrape his head.

"So this Rafe was dead?" Émile asked.

"Yes," I answered, acting like I was so out of it that I could barely stay on my feet.

"And you were the only one left behind?"

Trick question. Émile was better at grilling than Géant. I wasn't supposed to know about the graves downstream. Did he know about base camp? Did he know about Ethan and Cindy?

"As far as I know," I said. "I didn't see anyone else until I saw Mom."

Émile stared at me, letting my answer, or lie, float in the darkening cave entrance for several seconds. He glanced at Mom, then said something to Géant in French. Géant shrugged and said something back. I looked at Mom; her face was blank, neutral, like she was waiting for a verdict. And I guess she was.

"You should not have come here," Émile said.

Another man squeezed into the cavern through an opening in the back. He was thin and dark, and older than Émile and Géant. One of the Afghans. He had a rifle slung over his shoulder, a pistol strapped to his waist, and a headlamp around his forehead. He looked at me, then at Émile, as if he were waiting for instructions. Émile didn't say a word. Instead, he moved over to the left side of the cavern and turned on a battery-operated lantern hanging on the end of a rope. Along the wall beneath the lantern were four unrolled sleeping bags and a big pile of climbing gear—not as nice as the gear Plank had given us, but serviceable. Ethan wasn't going to be able to use this entrance to get into the cave. It would be like walking into a nest of venomous snakes. But I couldn't tell him, not then. The thing Ethan might hear next was me getting killed.

Émile picked up a pack of cigarettes off a sleeping bag, shook one out, and lit it. Gauloises. The Afghan guy followed suit and lit up too. Marlboro. Émile walked over to the narrow cave entrance and looked out into the darkness. By the time he turned back around, the cigarette was smoked halfway down. He said something to Marlboro Man in what I assumed was Pashtun. Marlboro stubbed his cigarette out on the wall, unslung his rifle, and nodded at Mom to go through the crack in the back wall.

"Let's go," she said, picking up a gallon of water.

I fell in behind her and stepped through the crack. It looked like this dead man was going to live another night. We made our way down a dark, narrow tunnel. At the end, maybe a hundred feet away, was another light. We passed three small openings on the right and two on the left, all big enough for someone to slip through. The first opening on the left had cool air coming out of it. The light at the end of the tunnel came from another Afghan. He was sitting on a blanket shuffling a deck of cards in lantern light. He gave me only a cursory glance as Marlboro pushed me through the opening at the end of the tunnel, which led to another tunnel about four feet long. Mom and I had to turn sideways to get to the cavern where the others were being held.

Alessia was on her feet in an instant. She ran across the cavern and threw her arms around me. Everyone started talking at once, but all I could hear was Alessia, because she was talking in my ear.

"We were so worried . . . We hoped you had gotten away

. . . I am sorry to see you here . . . This is all my fault . . . Elham, Ebadullah, Aki, Choma, Phillip, all dead because of me . . ."

I held her at arm's length. Tears were flowing down her cheeks. "It's not your fault." I nodded toward the opening. "It's their fault."

"But they are French."

I shook my head. "They are murderers."

JR, Will, and Jack came over and patted my back. The only person missing was Zopa. I looked around the dim cavern. He was sitting next to a wall with his knees up, smiling. He was the only one who didn't seem surprised to see me. I gave him a nod. He nodded back.

"Where's Rafe?"

"What about Ethan and Cindy?"

"How'd you find us?"

"Were you able to get word out?"

"Let's keep our voices down," Mom said, pointing at the entrance. "We're not sure if they speak English."

This quieted everyone down. I took off my pack and sat down next to Zopa, which was the farthest spot away from the entrance.

Alessia was going to sit next to me, then looked at Mom. "Please, you sit there."

Mom smiled. "No, go ahead."

The others sat down close and listened as I told them what had happened since I saw them last.

"We thought you were playing possum in the cave," JR said. "We were hoping you were on your way to get help."

"It would have taken days to get help," I said. "Rafe and

Cindy are on their way downriver in Ethan's kayak. The nearest village is at least three days away, providing they don't swamp the kayak, which looked like a definite possibility when they pushed off."

"I hope they don't run into Pierre," Jack said.

"Who's Pierre?"

"The third Frenchman," Mom answered. "I told you about him. He and the third Afghan left yesterday with the video."

I looked at JR. He had his head down. "They made us film the—"

"You didn't have a choice," I said, then looked at Jack. "Let's get back to this Pierre guy."

"They have a boat," Jack said.

"Probably two boats," Will added.

"Zopa's been eavesdropping on our guards," Mom said. "They don't know that he speaks Pashtun."

I looked at Zopa. He hadn't said a word since I got there.

"My Pashtun is far from perfect," he said. "But I believe they have two boats. Pierre, as we call him, is on his way to Kabul to make their demands. They want to have everything arranged and be gone from the area before the helicopter is scheduled to pick us up. He's not coming back here. The man he is with will return and tell the others that the negotiation was successful and it is time to leave. They are using complete radio and cell silence while they are here. Everyone left their phones in the boats. The second boat is for escape if the need arises, or to transport hostages. But of course there will be no hostages. They have no intention of letting any of us live."

I hoped Ethan was getting all this—

Idiot! There were no guards in the cavern. There was no reason to keep the two-way strapped to my side. There was no reason why I couldn't actually ask him if he *was getting all this.*

"Check the entrance," I said to Mom.

"The radio," she said.

She crawled over to the entrance, listened a moment, then turned and whispered, "The second guard is with the first. It sounds like they're playing cards."

I stripped my T-shirt off and began unwrapping the bandage. "Does anyone have earbuds?"

Three pairs appeared almost immediately. Jack's earbuds had a microphone. Mom stayed near the entrance. The others gathered round and shielded me in case a guard came into the cavern, which they said happened from time to time. I pulled the tape off the radio, plugged in the buds, and hit the talk button.

"Can you hear me?"

There was a slight hesitation, then a whispered *"Yeah, I can hear you."*

"What about earlier?"

"Most of it . . . I think."

"Where are you?"

"In a tree. Line of sight. Good tip from your mom. Probably seventy-five yards from the cave. Pretty much parallel. I'm looking through binoculars. It's dark. Can't see very well, but there's a guy standing just inside the entrance smoking a cigarette. I can see the ash glow."

"That might be Émile."

"What kind of shape are these guys in?"

"Excellent."

"What kind of weapons do they have?"

"Automatic rifles, pistols, knives, maybe other stuff I don't know about. You can't use the entrance. There are at least two guys there all of the time. There's a tunnel at the back of the entrance that leads to the small cavern we're in. Maybe a hundred feet long. There's an Afghan guard, sometimes two, outside the cavern all the time. Right now there are two. They're playing cards."

"Is the tunnel lit?"

"No. The guards use headlamps and have a lantern. There are five small openings in the tunnel. Two on the left, three on the right. I felt cool air coming from the first opening on the left heading toward the cavern we're in."

"How far is that opening from the guard?"

I had to think about that for a moment. "I'd guess sixty feet, maybe a little more."

"I guess it's ninja time for me. There has to be another way into the cave system. These guys are pros. They'd never put themselves into a dead-end hole. Does anybody know how they chose the hideout? They certainly didn't stumble across it. They had to know it was there."

I wasn't sure why this was important, but I asked the group. Zopa answered. He'd obviously spent a lot of time listening at the crack.

"It was a terrorist hideout during the war," he explained. "Émile was on the team that raided it."

I passed this on to Ethan.

"Definitely has to be another way in. I'll try to find it. Ask

someone what the guard situation is. What happens at bedtime? With some luck, I might be able to take one of them out, but not two of them."

Zopa said they usually played cards until ten or eleven, then one of them went up to the front cavern to sleep. He thought they were on roughly four-hour guard schedules. I told Ethan.

"One more question. How are the Afghans dressed?"

"Traditional Afghan clothes."

"Perfect. It will probably take me a while to get inside. Tell everyone they might want to get some sleep if they can. If we pull this off, the only thing we'll have going for us is a head start. We'll have to move fast and hard until we find help, which could be several days. I'll keep you posted. Out."

Now it was all up to the guy who had topped McKinley, ridden a snowboard down, and gotten chased by a wolf.

IF

Nobody is sleeping. We are looking at Phillip's maps and drone photos, which Géant didn't think were dangerous and let me keep. That was a mistake. The maps and photos are dangerous. They'll get us to Kabul if Ethan manages to get us out of here. Zopa thinks we should split up. Four people in two groups taking two routes. "Divide and conquer," he says. "Two chasing us is better than four, and eight cannot travel as fast as four." It makes sense to me. It makes sense to everyone. But who's on which team? This is why we are looking at the maps . . .

"THE GORGE BENEATH the plateau," Mom said, pointing at one of the drone photos. "This must be where the boat is."

"If there is a second boat," Jack said.

"And if there isn't a boat, you'll have to climb back up the gorge and go overland," JR said. "Doesn't look like there's a shoreline in the gorge. It will take the gorge group a day or two longer to get to base camp than the other group. If they can get there at all. Look at that terrain."

He was right about the river gorge and the terrain.

"It looks like the photo was taken on Mars," Will said.

"I think the boat is there," Mom said. "There is no way that Émile and Géant would allow themselves to be stranded here if things don't go well in Kabul with Pierre.

We'd be able to get downriver quickly and pick the other team up."

"And if we had the only boat, they'd never catch us," I added.

If there was a boat. *If* Ethan found the other entrance. *If* we got past the guard . . .

"Technical climb," Zopa said, pointing his thick index finger at the photo.

What he was saying was that it would be a dangerous climb. There were two drone photos of the river gorge. A close shot and a long shot. The long shot showed a twisting gash a hundred and fifty feet across, a couple miles long, and maybe a couple thousand feet deep. The close shot showed a smooth face with hardly any holds. We didn't have enough rope to get down to the river. We'd have to do it in stages. It other words, it was going to be a very ugly descent. If there wasn't a boat and we had to climb back up, it was going to be even uglier.

"You think they climbed this?" I asked.

Mom shook her head. "Not all of them. Géant and Émile are fit, but I don't think they're climbers. The same with our two guards. All four of them have relatively soft hands. My guess is that Pierre and his Afghan partner, who definitely looked like climbers, dropped the others off downriver to make their way overland, then motored up to the gorge, stashed the boats, then made the ascent."

"Why not leave the boats downriver?" JR asked.

"No place to hide them from the eye in the sky," Mom said. "No cover along the river. A surveillance drone would pick out a boat along the barren shore in an instant." She pointed at the gorge. "This is the only place to hide boats."

"So who's going where?" Will asked.

"Nobody is going anywhere unless we get out of here," Mom said. "But if we do manage to escape, I think the climb master should make the call." She looked at Zopa.

Zopa looked at me. "How is Ethan's ankle?"

I'd forgotten he'd injured it. He hadn't limped since we had gotten to the stream. "Healed, I think."

"Good. Peak, me, Teri, and Alessia will descend the gorge. JR, Will, Jack, and Ethan will meet us downriver."

I think I saw relief in the film crew's faces. I wondered what Ethan would think of Zopa's team division.

"How long do we wait at the river?" Jack asked.

"You don't wait for us," Zopa answered. "You keep moving. The only thing you'll carry is water and some food. Speed will be everything. We can stay in touch with the two-way radios when we are close enough. We will take your climbing equipment with us. Everything else stays here."

"What if we can't reach you on the radio?" JR asked.

"You keep moving downriver," Zopa said. "The goal is for someone to survive this."

IT TOOK US OVER AN HOUR to sort and divide the gear, which was good because it took our minds off Ethan's progress, or lack thereof. We hadn't heard a word from him since he signed off. Our team split the water between us. Ethan's team (that's how I thought of them) didn't need water because they'd be able to replenish at the stream before they tackled the hill. According to the maps and photos, our team would be heading away from the stream and wouldn't be able to get water until we reached the river at the bottom of the gorge. And to be honest, the water at the bottom of the gorge had me a bit worried because I couldn't swim. I brought this little snag up with Zopa and Mom, suggesting that maybe I should go with the film crew and Ethan should go with them. Of course, in a small cavern, there is no such thing as privacy. Everyone got in on the conversation.

"You cannot swim?" Alessia asked.

Great.

"I can't swim either," Mom admitted. "We'll go down together," she added.

"I don't want to climb down that gorge," Will said. "And no offense, Peak, but I'd rather take my chance with an ex-marine, even if it means crossing the open scree again."

"No offense taken."

"Can you swim?" Alessia asked Zopa.

He shook his head. "Not many opportunities for a Sherpa to swim in the Himalayas."

"As narrow as that gorge is," Jack said, "I doubt an Olympic swimmer would be able to tread water in those rapids. In fact, if there is a boat, it will be interesting keeping it under control."

That was a comforting thought.

"Not a problem," Mom said. "When I was young, I made my climbing money leading white-water rafting trips."

Yet another thing I didn't know about her.

"You said you couldn't swim," Jack said.

"And you said no one could tread water in the gorge,

and you're right. But that holds true for almost all rapids. We wore life vests. It's probably too much to hope for, but I hope the boat is fully equipped with life vests. Be assured, I will be the first—" She glanced at me. "Make that the second person to strap one on."

I heard someone whispering in my ear. I'd forgotten that I'd left one of the buds in to listen for Ethan. I waved everyone to be quiet and pressed the talk button.

"I'm here."

"*Me too . . . or almost. The second entrance is on top. There's an old ladder that leads down to the tunnels. Pretty easy to follow because they've been using the entrance. Before I poke my head into your tunnel, I need to know where your guard is, what he's doing, and if he's alone.*"

"Hang on. This might take a while."

"*I have all the time in the world.*"

I explained the situation to the others, saying that I would go down the short tunnel to check on the guards.

"I'm skinnier than you are," Will said. "I'll go."

"Are you sure?" I asked.

"No," Will answered. "Turn off the lights."

We turned the lanterns off. For a second, dim light filtered through the entrance, then the cavern went completely black as Will squeezed through the narrow crack. If Will made a sound, if the guard, or guards, looked up at the wrong time, our escape hopes would be all over, and there was a good chance Will would be dead.

There was no sound except for our breathing. My eyes began to water from staring at the black entrance. I looked at my watch. A minute went by, then two, then three . . . Six minutes after he started, the dim light reappeared through the crack.

"Turn the lights on," Will said.

He was drenched in sweat. I was too.

"He's alone," Will said. "Playing solitaire. Cards on his blanket. Facing the long tunnel. Headlamp on. His rifle is leaned against the wall. Pistol still strapped to his waist . . . I think." He grabbed a water bottle and drained it.

I passed the information on to Ethan in a whisper.

"Copy that. Wish he was asleep. Guess I'll just have to try the frontal approach."

"What do you mean?"

"Pop out into the tunnel wearing Afghan garb. Blind him with my headlamp. Hope he thinks I'm his partner. Take him out without making a sound. Simple. This is going to take a while. I'm at the base of the ladder so they can't hear me. Stand by. Be ready to split. Make sure you tie down all the gear so it doesn't rattle in the tunnel. Out."

The two-way went silent. His rattle suggestion was a good one. My gear was already cinched down. It took fifteen minutes to silence everyone else's gear. When we finished, we simply stood there with our packs on, staring at the crack in the wall, listening. Several more minutes passed.

"Did you hear that?" JR whispered.

I hadn't heard anything. I looked at the others. All of them were shaking their heads.

"A thump," JR said. "I swear I—"

Someone was coming through the entrance. He was wearing a headlamp, a rifle slung over his shoulder, a pistol tucked into his Afghan pants. Ethan. His easy smile was gone, as if he had never smiled in his life. He had blood on his hands.

"Follow me," he whispered, harshly. "Not a word, not a cough until we get up top. Turn your headlamps off."

I was the last to leave the cavern. I looked to my left as I stepped out of the entrance. Our guard was sitting on his blanket. His headlamp was pointed down at a deck of bloody cards.

UP TOP

It's a maze of tunnels, right, left, left, right . . . I'm completely turned around. I'm surprised Ethan remembers the way, but he does. We stop in a narrow tunnel, single file. Ethan sheds his Afghan disguise. One at a time, we climb a rickety wooden ladder, maybe twenty feet up. I'm the last to pop through the rabbit hole. We are in a grove of trees. It's dark and cool. It feels good to be free, but the hard part is still to come . . .

ETHAN CLOSED a crudely built trapdoor over the hole in the ground.

"Get some rocks and logs," he said. "I'd like to disable this exit if we can."

We piled everything we could find on top of the door.

"That ought to hold them," Ethan said. "At least for a while. What's the plan?"

Mom quickly rolled out a map and explained what we had in mind.

"Makes good sense," Ethan said, without a word about the team divisions or anything else. "How much time do you think we have?"

Mom looked at her watch. "The second guard has been relieving the first guard around six. It's a little after two now. So we may have four hours."

"They're going to know we used this trapdoor," Ethan

said. "But it'll take them a while to get up here. We're about fifty feet above the main entrance. They either have to climb up the wall or go around. From what you say about their climbing abilities, I think they'll go around if there aren't other exits. The question is, are they going to split up and send one guy after one group and two guys after the other? Hopefully we'll be so far ahead of them that we'll never find out." He looked at me. "Do you want the pistol or the rifle?"

I didn't want either of them. I'd never fired a gun in my life.

Mom stepped forward. "Pistol," she said.

Ethan handed it to her. "Do you know how to use it?"

Mom answered by pulling the slide back, jacking a round into the chamber, and flipping the safety on.

French, she knows how to operate a boat, and she knows how to use a gun.

"Guess we'll keep the radios on the same channel they're on now," Ethan said.

"How'd you find this entrance?" I asked.

Ethan grinned for the first time since leaving the cave. "It was kind of weird. It took me an hour to get up here. I was sure that if there was a back door, this was the place. An hour later I wasn't so sure. I was about ready to give up and try a different area when I saw something move into this grove of trees and stop. Or I thought I saw something. Anyway, I started walking this way, and I saw that cat you were talking about."

"The snow leopard?"

"I don't know if it was the same one or not. Can't be too many of them around, though. It was sitting on top of the trapdoor. I'm not kidding. Maybe it smelled food or something coming up from the tunnels."

"Or maybe it was something else," I said, although I wasn't sure what that something else might be.

"Maybe," Ethan said. "I'm just glad it did. I wouldn't have come into this grove. I thought it was too far from the entrance for a back door." He looked at his watch. "We better get footing it. With some luck, we'll see you downriver."

We shook hands and hugged. Ethan's team headed southwest. Our team headed northeast.

ZOPA INSISTED that Mom and Alessia take the lead, saying that he wanted to talk to me. They set a pretty fast pace through the forest, which I tried to match, but Zopa held me back. It turned out he didn't want to talk, he wanted me to help him obscure "the tiny boot prints" Mom and Alessia were leaving in the soft ground. We shuffled more than walked. Mom and Alessia pulled farther and farther ahead. I didn't care if Zopa wanted to talk or not. I had things to say.

"You knew we were going to show up at the cave," I said.

Zopa shook his head. "I knew you would try to reach the cave. I did not know about Ethan or his unique skills. That was good fortune."

"Not for the guy he killed."

"Karma. The man who died is the one who murdered Choma, Aki, and Phillip. But all of them carry responsibility."

"You should have told Ethan that," I said. "I think he was upset about killing him."

"If you kill someone, or something, you should feel regret."

"Ethan didn't have a choice."

"Of course he had a choice. He made the choice that most benefited his needs and ours. Émile and the others made the choices that most benefited their wants."

"Are you saying they're justified in what they did?"

"You were not listening," Zopa scolded. "I said needs and wants. They are not the same thing. They *want* money. Their desire for this justifies anything and everything. We *need* to survive. Our desire for this justifies almost anything and everything."

"Almost?" I asked.

"The difference between wants and needs is very slight. It is slippery. It is often difficult to tell the difference between the two."

"I'll have to think about that when I'm not fleeing for my life."

Zopa laughed. "Yes, that is probably best."

"What about the *shen*?"

"Now, that is a true mystery and something I will have to think about when I'm back at the monastery and not fleeing for my life."

"Probably just a coincidence," I said.

"Ha! Probably just a living talisman. There are no coincidences. Everything that happens has purpose, which is another thing you can think about when you are not fleeing for your life. Ethan joining us with his unique skill set was not a coincidence. He thought he was here to climb a mountain, but he was sent for a very different reason.

Everyone and everything has a part to play in this, but none of us will know the full extent of what that part is."

We nearly bumped into Mom and Alessia, who had stopped to wait for us.

"What are you two talking about?" Mom asked. "We're feeling a little left out."

"Talismans, want versus need, fleeing for our lives, destiny—just the regular stuff," I said.

Alessia smiled, although I wasn't sure she'd understood everything I had just said. We stepped out of the trees onto a plateau of barren rock lit by the waning moon. I looked at my watch. The GPS was down again. We'd been walking for two hours.

"At least it's not scree," Mom said. "Have you seen Pierre's footprints?"

Zopa shook his head. "He might have come a different way. Finding where he descended should be easy once we reach the gorge."

Which was about fifteen miles away, if we'd calculated our position correctly.

"I'm just glad we're traveling at night," Mom said. "Walking across this plateau during the day would be like walking on molten lava, but I guess it's better than—" She stopped in midsentence and fixed her headlamp on Zopa. "How many men do you think are coming this way?"

"I think two of them. Émile and Géant. But only if there's a second boat or if they pick up Alessia's footprints, which I think we've managed to cover up pretty well." He looked off across the plateau. "They won't be able to track us on this hard rock, but they don't have to. If they know we came this way, they know we are after their boat. That is the fastest way downriver. They have no more desire to cross the scree than we do. The boat is their best hope of catching us or getting away if they fail. I think they will send the remaining guard after Ethan's team. Émile and Géant will try to get to the boat and cut them off."

"But they aren't climbers," I said.

"Perhaps not," Zopa said. "But they are desperate. They will do anything to capture us or get away."

THE PELT

The sun is up. It's early morning. The gorge is nowhere in sight. Mom has the map spread out on the rocky ground. I can't say we're lost, because we didn't exactly know where we were in the first place. Everyone is pointing at the map and talking at once. Even Zopa is getting a little tense. This reminds me of the daily where-do-you-want-to-go-for-dinner conversations back in New York, which reminds me of the twins and Rolf, who have no idea how horrible our little vacation in "After Can Stand" has been, and they won't know for several days. That is, if we survive. I back away from the debate and find a nice boulder to sit on. Alessia glances over her shoulder. A moment later, she joins me, leaving Mom and Zopa to figure out what to do next . . .

"IT IS TOO bad the GPS does not work," she said.

"That would solve a lot of problems," I said, amazed at how great she looked after the kidnapping, the long trek across the scree, the deaths, the dank cavern, more death, and our escape. She wasn't as perfect as she had been when I first saw her rappel down the cliff face, but she was pretty close. She had resiliency, which was something I wished I had more of.

"What will you do when this is over?" she asked.

It was all I could do not to point out that this was far from over, and that I might not be able to do anything, because I might not be alive. She might not be alive either.

"I'll go home," I found myself saying. "New York."

"We go to New York," she said. "Every year. For Christmas. My mother and I."

"You'll have to come and see us. Meet my twin sisters."

"You have sisters?"

"Patrice and Paula. Seven years old. I miss them."

"Your mother must be missing them as well."

"She hasn't said anything, but I'm sure she's going out of her mind with worry."

That's when it occurred to me that Mom probably hadn't said anything about the twins, or Rolf, because if she did, she might completely lose it. Her advice to me when I was on Everest was to be selfish and to think only about the climb. *Your guts and heart need to be stone cold,* she had said.

"It might be good not to say anything to her about the twins," I suggested.

"I understand," Alessia said.

I glanced over at Mom. She was rolling up the map. They must have come to an agreement.

"*Vautours,*" Alessia said, pointing.

I didn't understand the word, but I recognized what she was pointing at. Circling over the plateau, maybe a mile away, were at least a dozen vultures. I remembered what Ethan had said about the three graves along the stream. There was something dead on the plateau.

Zopa looked over at us. "It's on our way," he said.

• • •

AT FIRST WE COULDN'T TELL if it was an animal or a human. A few of the vultures had landed and were feeding on it. As we drew closer, the vultures started to flap away.

"It is a snow leopard," Alessia whispered.

At first I didn't see how she could tell. All I saw was a pile of flesh the size of a medium dog. It could be anything. But she wasn't talking about the pile, she was looking at something beyond the pile, something horrible. Stretched taut on a crudely made rack was a snow leopard pelt. Ethan had seen the snow leopard the night before. The men couldn't have gotten in front of us and shot it.

"It is not the same snow leopard," Zopa said. "It may be the mate of the one who has been watching over us. It is several days old."

"But who did it and why?" I shouted, furious.

It wasn't as if I wasn't angry about the other deaths. I was. But seeing the skin drying in the morning sun pushed me over the edge. I'd had enough of stupid deaths.

Alessia put her hand on my arm. I thought about jerking away. I didn't want to be comforted. I wanted to kill the guy who had done this and stretch his skin out on crude poles. I wanted *vautours* to feed on his flesh. I wanted to—

"As to who did this," Zopa said, "it was probably one of the kidnappers. One of the Afghans, I would guess."

"But why?"

"Ten thousand dollars in Russia," Alessia said. "Maybe more. Poaching is a huge problem here. It declined during the war, which increased the price for pelts."

"How do you know that?"

"My father was a conservation biologist."

"Was?"

"He died," she said. "In the Congo when I was ten years old. Killed by rebels, they say, but my mother believes he was murdered by the gorilla poachers he was trying to stop."

I took a deep breath, trying to calm myself. Seeing this had to be a lot worse for her than it was for me.

"I'm sorry," I said.

"He was a wonderful man," Alessia said.

"Maybe we should take the skin down," I said.

"I'm certain whoever did this intended to pick it up on his way back through," Zopa said.

"The one who did this might already be dead back in the cave," I said. This idea made me feel a little better, but Mom shot this happy thought down.

"I don't think so," she said. "The man in the cave wasn't a climber. This had to have been done by the man with Pierre, or maybe Pierre himself. The others didn't come this way."

"Why didn't they take the skin with them when they came back through here?" I asked.

"They were in a hurry," Alessia said. "And the skin is still green and heavy."

"We will leave it where it is," Zopa said. "We at least know that they walked this way."

Zopa was right. An hour and a half later, we reached the gorge.

THE EDGE

It's deep and sheer. Two thousand feet to the river. We walk along the edge, looking down, trying to figure out where they descended. Between us, we have four hundred feet of rope, which we will have to halve in order to retrieve the rope between pitches. We could tie the ropes together and take ten or twelve pitches down to the water. The problem with this is that everyone would have to hang on the wall until the last person on the rope reached them. I haven't seen a lot of great places to hang on the wall. The crumbly rock is a lot like hard dirt. Totally unstable, which is probably how the gorge was formed in the first place. The river cut through it like it was tissue. The alternative is for each of us to make our own way down. This means taking more than forty pitches each to get to the river. Harder, but maybe safer, because we would be able to choose our own descents, making adjustments on the way, depending on the condition of the rock. But first we have to find out where and how Pierre tackled the problem. In an odd way, he's the climb master now . . .

"HERE!" ALESSIA SHOUTED.

We joined her. She was standing next to a shiny new anchor.

Zopa got down on his knees and reefed on the anchor several times. It didn't budge. "Long shafted," he said. "It will hold. If we choose to use it."

That was the question, and I could see by everyone's expression we were all wondering the same thing. I got on my stomach and looked over the edge. It was a long way down. Twice the height of the New York Times building, which I had climbed when I was an idiot. The difference was that the fifty-two-story Times building was made out of solid steel and glass. The gorge was rotten rock all the way down. I did see some small ledges here and there, that might have allowed some purchase to reset the rope, but there weren't many of them, and it was impossible to tell how solid they were. I was about to get up and report back to the others, but saw they were all lying next to me, heads over the edge, checking it out for themselves. I didn't blame them. I'd never take someone else's word for a descent. Especially one as hairy as this.

We stood and were about to start the descent discussion when a bullet answered the question for us. It ricocheted off the ground right between Mom and me. We hit the deck instantly, along with Alessia and Zopa.

"Did you see where it came from?"

"Is anyone hurt?"

"How'd they get here so quickly?"

No one had seen where it came from, no one was hurt, and no one had any idea how they, if it was *they*, had gotten there so quickly. They must have discovered the dead guard earlier than expected. Another bullet hit the ground, but farther away than the first. Probably because we were lying down now and not silhouetted against the gorge.

"I saw it this time." Mom pointed. "A thousand yards. Two of them."

I saw them. Two big figures jogging our way. It had to be Émile and Géant. One of the figures stopped, fired a round, then resumed jogging.

"Pound in anchors," Zopa said. "Everyone over the side."

"We'll never make it in time if we don't slow them down," Mom shouted, pulling the pistol out of her waistband. "I can't hit them with this, but I can get them to take cover." To prove her point, she fired a shot. Both men hit the ground. "I'll use the anchor Pierre set after you've all started down."

"I'll set your rope," I said.

"No, Peak!"

I ignored her and pulled the rope out of her pack. As I attached it to the anchor, I heard her fire another shot.

"That didn't slow them down!" Mom shouted. "They're running toward us now."

"How far?" Zopa asked.

"Five hundred yards," Mom answered.

Zopa had his anchor in and was fixing his rope. Alessia was a step ahead of him. She was clipping her harness around her waist.

"Four hundred yards," Mom said.

I started pounding my anchor in.

"Three hundred yards," Mom said.

"Fire at them," I said, feeding my rope into the anchor.

"They know I can't hit them from here. That's why they're up and running. I need to wait for them to get closer."

I fixed my rope, then crawled over to Mom and pulled her harness out of her pack.

"Just go!" she said.

"Plenty of time," I said with more calm than I felt. "I'm just going to get your harness set."

Émile and Géant were now two hundred yards away, almost sprinting across the plateau. The only things slowing them down were their rifles and their heavy packs, which were both loaded with climbing gear. I looked over at Zopa. He and Alessia were hooked into their harnesses, squatting on the edge with their backs to the gorge.

"You see the gear?" I shouted.

Zopa nodded. "They'll come down after us."

I was more worried about them cutting our ropes before we were able to pull them and get rigged for our second pitch.

I think Zopa understood that too. "We have to go."

"We'll be right behind you." I looked at Alessia. She was obviously frightened and worried. I tried to give her a confident smile, but I'm not sure she saw it before she and Zopa disappeared over the lip of the gorge.

"Hundred yards," Mom said, the pistol still pointed at the men.

"Your harness is set. You need to get into it. We have to go."

"Two seconds." She took a deep breath, let it out slowly, then squeezed the trigger.

One of the men went down. I think it was Géant. Émile went flat and returned fire. He started to get back up. Mom fired again. She didn't hit him, but the shot ricocheted on a rock near his right leg. He hit the ground again.

"Time to go," Mom said.

We backed our way to the gorge and dropped over the edge.

THE GORGE

I rope down about forty feet and stop. There's a toehold just big enough for me to catch while I pull the rope and reset. Zopa and Alessia are about fifty feet below me to my right, setting up for their second pitch. Mom stops ten feet above me, a little to my left. We both have more rope, but it's best to rerig when you can, not where the rope ends. And then there's Émile. If he gets to our anchors before we pull our ropes, he'll cut us loose—

"ROCK!" MOM SHOUTED.

I hugged the wall and covered my head. I'd left my helmet on the hillside with the camel. It wasn't a rock. It was her pistol. It hit me in the shoulder, painfully. I made a grab for it, but missed.

"Drop something?" A man's voice shouted from above.

Émile. He was on his stomach, hanging out over the edge, pointing his rifle at us. "If any of you descends one more inch, I will shoot all of you."

I doubted he would shoot Alessia, but I had no doubt that he'd shoot me and the others. He didn't even have to waste a bullet on Mom and me. All he had to do was reach out with a knife and cut our ropes. It was probably lucky Mom had dropped the pistol. If she hadn't, she would be falling right now. Climbing back up to Émile was not going to be easy, but that wasn't what he had in mind.

He called down to Mom. "Retrieve your rope, or I'll cut your son's rope."

Mom hooked on to the wall and pulled her rope.

"You next," he said, pointing his rifle at me.

I retrieved my rope.

"I am coming down. We will descend together. Slowly. If I tell you to stop. You will stop. If you do not. I will shoot you. Do you understand?"

I nodded, and I'm sure the others did too. The wall was as flat as the side of a glass building. There was no place to hide.

"I am going to attach my rope now. When I look back over the edge, if any of you have moved, I will shoot you."

He didn't ask us if we understood this time; he just disappeared. We stayed exactly where we were. There was nothing we could do. There was obviously a second boat, and he wanted to get to it. A couple minutes later, a rope flew over the edge. A few seconds after that, Émile roped down with his rifle slung over his shoulder, stopping about ten feet above Mom. He may not have been climbing recently. Soft hands. But judging by the way he had rigged his harness and descended, he knew what he was doing. There was no sign of Géant. Mom had either killed him or wounded him so badly, he couldn't join us. I wished she had shot Émile instead.

"Small increments all the way to the river," Émile said. "You will wait for me to retrieve my rope, then reset. No one descends until I tell you to. When I say stop, everyone stops or everyone gets shot. Go."

Of course, Émile stopped when he had something to

grab on to or a toehold. We stopped when he told us to, which meant that most of the time we had nothing to hang on to but our ropes. To avoid this problem, I picked a spot below that looked like it had something I could latch on to, then slowed down or sped up my descent, trying to time it for when Émile shouted for us to stop. This took my mind off the fact there was a French maniac rappelling down behind me with a gun pointed at my head. The only hope we had was that he would screw up and fall to his death. I nearly got my wish halfway down the cliff when his rope got jammed.

"Stop!"

At first I didn't know what was going on. He'd only descended about fifteen feet from his anchor and was dangling in a terrible spot. From where I was, I couldn't see anything for him to grab on to.

"He's stuck," Mom said. She was the closest to him.

So what? I wanted to say. *Let him dangle.* It was scary, but relatively safe if your anchor held, which I hoped his didn't. The way out of it was to climb back up the rope to the anchor and reset your rope. Of course Émile's problem was a little more complex than that, because when you're climbing up, you have to look up. Hard to do when you're trying to point a rifle down at your climbing partners or, in our case, his climbing targets.

"Old man! Get up here and help me!" There wasn't any panic in his voice. Just extreme irritation.

Zopa was the farthest away from him.

"I'll do it," I said. "I'm closer, and I have a good route up to you."

It wasn't a great route, but it was better than Zopa's or Mom's, although she was even closer to him than I was.

"Yes," Émile said. "You do it."

As I climbed up, I wondered if I would have the courage to drop him if I got the chance. I stopped to rest and glanced down at the others. Everyone was looking up at me, but none more intently than Zopa. His dark eyes were locked on to me like lasers. He shook his head as if he knew what I was thinking and wanted me to stop thinking it. Was my thinking a *want* or a *need?* Clearly Zopa felt it was a want. But I wasn't so sure. Weren't there times when a want and a need were the same thing?

"Get up here," Émile growled.

"I'm coming," I said.

But I hadn't decided if I was going to kill him or not. I climbed up next to him. He was dangling like a spider on the end of a thread about six feet out from the wall. His rope had fallen over an outcrop, which was why he was hanging so far from the wall when he got jammed. It was an amateurish mistake. Maybe Émile wasn't the climber I had thought he was. If I'd had a knife, all I'd have had to do was touch the rope with the blade and he'd have been gone. I didn't have a knife. Or the will. But I was working on that. I glanced back down at Zopa. He was still zeroed in on me.

Yeah, yeah, I hear you, cagey monk.

I peered up at Émile's anchor. It looked like the rope had doubled over and knotted as it slipped through the carabiner. I'd need slack to get it loose.

Émile had unslung his rifle and was pointing it down in the general direction of Mom, with his finger on the trigger.

He was smiling, trying to act like dangling a thousand feet above a river was no big deal, but I could tell he was nervous about it.

"What will you do?"

"Pull you to the wall, anchor you, climb up and untangle your rope, and drop it down to you."

"Do it," he said.

It was easier to explain it than it was to *do it*, but I managed. After getting him hooked to the wall on a new anchor, I climbed to the top of the outcrop and paused to catch my breath. He'd insisted on keeping his original rope tied to his harness, saying he wanted it there for safety. I think he wanted it tied to the harness in case he butterfingered the rope when I dropped it down to him. I glanced down at his rope and realized that if I grabbed it, I might be able to make him dance like a marionette, maybe even hard enough to make him drop the rifle. I might even be able to dislodge the anchor holding him and drop him into the river. I looked down at Zopa. Mistake. He was still locked on to me. He gave me another head shake. I didn't believe he was reading my mind. I thought he was putting himself in my place, knowing that he'd be tempted to rope-a-dope Émile too. The dope with the gun was moving his weapon from head to head. I didn't think he'd be able to hit anyone intentionally as I was shaking him, but if he managed to hang on to the rifle and hold the trigger down, he might hit someone accidentally. It was a risk, but a risk that might be worth taking.

"What's taking so long?" Émile shouted.

"Just looking for a handhold," I said.

Debating whether I should try to kill you, I thought.

Zopa had stopped shaking his head. For a second I thought he was giving me the go-ahead—not that I needed his permission—but no such luck. It looked like he was nodding at something to his right. I scanned the cliff face. There was nothing I could—

The *shen* was back, not thirty feet away from me. The ledge it was standing on was no wider than my boot. It actually looked like it was floating in thin air. I quickly turned my head. I didn't want Émile to see it. For all I knew, Émile had shot the other snow leopard. Our guesses about how they got here were pure speculation. Émile had made some dumb mistakes during this climb, but he wasn't without skill. He could have come up this way originally with the help of someone who knew what he was doing. I scrambled up to his anchor.

"I need some slack!" I yelled.

Émile sent some my way, and I had him untangled in an instant. I dropped the rope down to him, hooked on to the anchor, and lowered myself with regret.

THE DARKENING

I'm convinced that we are no longer hostages. That Émile has no intention of releasing us, whether the ransom is paid or not. He is using us to get down the cliff. This is the only reason we are alive. He gets tangled two more times. Zopa frees him, then Mom frees him. And each time, I'm disappointed. Émile lives. If he gets tangled again, I'm going to volunteer to free him. I'm going to . . . I'm not sure what I'll do, but I want another chance to decide.

"Stop!" Émile shouts.

We stop, dangle, wait for him to catch up. A sliver of light from the cliffs illuminates the gorge, but it's getting darker with every pitch.

The shen is still stalking us, pausing when we stop, moving when we drop, nearly invisible, always about thirty feet above, alighting like a gray moth on bits of rock and ledges I can't see. The only real climber among us is the shen . . .

I COULD HEAR the roar of the rapids two hundred feet below and see the black inflatable boat pulled up on a shelf cut into rock by the fast water. Alessia had been inching her way closer to me the last several pitches and was now only ten feet away. Her face was streaked with dirt and sweat, her black hair powdered with rock dust, her pale blue eyes bloodshot, her lips swollen and chapped. We'd finished the last of our water a thousand feet ago.

"Zopa says that we will be fine," she said.

I shrugged. I seriously doubted it, but I didn't want to tell her that.

"He told me that we would be saved from above," she said.

I glanced up. Émile was making his way down and had just about reached the end of his rope. Above him the *shen* was carefully picking its way down the wall. As terrible as our circumstances were and as exhausted as I was, I couldn't help but be amazed and awed by the cat's ability to balance on what looked like nothing.

"Do you think he meant God?" Alessia asked.

The question threw me. I didn't know what she was talking about, which must have shown on my face, because she gave me a gentle smile.

"Zopa," she said. "Do you think that by *above*, he meant that God would save us?"

"I don't know. It's sometimes hard to know what Zopa means. His idea of what *saved* means might be different from ours."

It was Alessia's turn to look confused. I gave her a cracked-lip smile. "I'm just saying that he doesn't think like you and I. He doesn't see things the same way. He's comfortable with mysteries like the *shen*."

"*Shen*?"

"Snow leopard. It's been following us all the way down the face."

"I didn't see a—" She started to look up.

"Don't look! I don't want Émile to see it."

Émile had reached the end of his pitch and was hammering in his next anchor.

"Go!" he shouted down at us.

Alessia and I started down side by side. The lower wall of the gorge was rougher than the upper part, with more hand- and footholds. We were able to rappel all the way to the ends of our ropes. Two more pitches, and we'd reach the river and find out if we'd be saved by something from above. I just hoped I'd be able to get a drink of water before we were murdered.

Once again, Alessia stopped right next to me, and Zopa stopped right next to her. Mom was about thirty feet to my left. Émile was coming down slowly above us.

"I still do not see the snow leopard," Alessia said.

"Thirty, maybe forty feet above Émile, to his left. Just make sure you look away when Émile stops."

"Oh, yes! I see it. It is *magnifique!*"

The *shen* was nearly sprinting down the face now. I was afraid Émile was going to see it, but once again, it stopped the instant Émile stopped, as if it knew who its enemy was.

"I'm out of anchors!" Émile shouted. "Bring me one."

He hadn't directed this to anyone in particular, but Mom was closest to him.

"Hang on," she said.

She started free climbing up to him. I guess he didn't realize that he could free climb too—we all could.

"There are enough holds to get down the last hundred feet to the river blindfolded," I said.

"Not if you want to use a rifle," Zopa said. "And not if you are an unskilled climber."

Both good points. I hadn't had a chance to talk to Zopa since he had warned me off trying to murder Émile, which I still thought was a mistake.

"He's just using us to get to the river," I said.

"No doubt," Zopa agreed.

"So what happens when he gets to the river?"

"He will try to kill us."

"Then why didn't you let me—"

"I said he would try," Zopa interrupted. "He will not succeed."

"You think the *shen* is going to attack him?" I asked sarcastically.

Sarcasm was about as effective on Zopa as it was on Alessia.

He looked confused, then said, "The *shen* is not here to save us. That is not the cat's role. *Shen*s are not violent creatures unless you are a deer or small mammal or a bird."

"Yeah, I get that, but you told Alessia that we would be saved from above."

"And I believe we will be. Do you remember the eagles?"

The eagle attack seemed like it had happened a hundred years earlier.

"I remember."

I also remembered that Zopa seemed to understand

what the birds were going to do before the birds knew they were going to do it, like some kind of raptor whisperer.

"The eagles are going to help us?"

Zopa shook his head. "Very doubtful. Eagles are territorial. I don't think they use this gorge."

"Then what—"

"You have been so focused on Émile and the *shen*, you have missed something. You have lost your focus. It happens. You will see what you missed when we reach the river."

I heard a familiar *ping* above. Émile was hammering in an anchor. Mom was nearly back to where she had started from. She was climbing easily and seemed pretty relaxed. I wondered if she had seen what Zopa said I had missed.

"Go!" Émile shouted.

Two more pitches, and we were on the ground, standing on shaky legs with the cliff in front of us, the river roaring behind. Émile hung twenty feet above, pointing his rifle down at us.

"You can unhook and drink," he said.

Which I think meant he wanted to get to the ground and unhook while we were a safe distance away, not that we were stupid enough to rush him. If we'd wanted to take him out, we would have done it on the face. I was still mad about that as I dropped my harness and walked over to the river to get a drink.

I put my head completely underwater. When I came up for air, I found I was sandwiched by Mom and Alessia, both shaking out their long wet hair. I scooped several handfuls of water into my parched mouth.

"What do you think Émile will do?" Alessia asked.

I thought he was going to shoot Mom, me, and Zopa in the back, tie Alessia up, and take her downriver. But I didn't tell her this. I shrugged.

Zopa had already slaked his thirst and was back on his feet facing the cliff. We got up and turned around. Émile was on the ground, unhooked, thirty feet away, pointing his rifle at us.

"The boat is not big enough for all of us," he said.

The boat was plenty big enough for all of us if one of us hadn't been a kidnapper worried that we would jump him in the confined space.

I looked at the cliff face. The *shen* was twenty feet above him, moving to his right, slowly descending. I wanted to shout and warn it off, but that would draw attention to the cat.

Émile put his rifle to his shoulder. I looked at Mom. Tears rolled down her cheeks. A sad smile on her face. She put her arms around me.

"Don't," Alessia pleaded.

"I am not going to shoot you," Émile said. "Step away from them."

"No!" Alessia grabbed Zopa and pulled him in to us.

It was a delaying tactic that wasn't going to work for very long, but it was worth it to see Émile's rage. I thought he was going to shoot Alessia too, but he didn't. He just stood there glaring.

"We could fall back into the river," I said quietly. "Take our chances."

"A cork couldn't survive in this water," Mom said.

"We will be fine," Zopa said. "Just stay where you are. Watch the *shen*."

The *shen* jumped from the wall to the shelf and started moving toward the inflatable boat. Émile swung his rifle toward it.

"No!" I shouted, breaking away from the group—

The shen *freezes in place and looks up at the sky. Émile points his rifle at me and grins. The gorge somehow gets darker, like a cloud is passing overhead, which is impossible. The gorge is too deep and narrow for sunlight to reach the river unless the sun is directly overhead. I wonder if this unnatural darkening is something that happens just before you die. I look back at Mom. She is moving toward me with her arms out, screaming. I hear a gunshot, then another, and another. I'm surprised it doesn't hurt. I look back at Émile . . .*

He was on the ground covered in blood.

FROM ABOVE

The shen bolts, bounding up the cliff face as if it's running across flat ground. Mom must have found the pistol she dropped. That's the only explanation . . . But it isn't . . . Ethan floats down to the shelf, releasing his paraglider chute two feet from the ground. The chute billows into the river and is swept away . . .

ETHAN DIDN'T TAKE his rifle off of Émile as he walked over to him. He kicked Émile's weapon away, then kneeled and felt for a pulse. It wasn't until he was sure Émile was gone that he looked at me and grinned.

"Guess you and I are back among the living," he said.

Mom and Alessia threw their arms around him. Zopa stood to the side, smiling.

"From above," I said.

Zopa shrugged.

"How did you know?"

I expected another shrug, but he surprised me. "I saw him. He looked over the edge of the cliff with a pair of binoculars. The sun caught a lens. He watched us for a long time. At first I thought he might climb down after us. When he didn't, I remembered his parachute."

"Paraglider," I said.

Zopa shrugged.

"How did you know it wasn't Géant?"

"He would have shouted down to Émile."

It all made perfect sense, and to be honest, I was a little disappointed. I didn't want it to make sense.

"He had to wait until we were on the ground," Zopa continued. "He had to time his jump perfectly." He looked up at the cliff. "And so did the *shen.*"

I looked up. The *shen* was two hundred feet up the cliff and moving quickly. I watched until the cat disappeared, then looked back at Zopa.

"What do you mean the *shen* timed its jump perfectly?"

"The jump to the shelf. A second earlier, or a second later, one of us would have noticed Ethan floating down and looked up. Émile might have followed our gaze and shot Ethan before Ethan could . . ." He nodded at Émile. "The *shen* was here to distract us. To hold our attention at the right moment."

I grinned. That was more like it.

THE BOAT WAS FILLED with supplies, including life vests and two satellite phones, which didn't work in the gorge. There were about four hours of daylight left.

"The water's fast," Mom said. "It won't take us more than twenty minutes to get out of the gorge. But we won't get out at all if I don't take some time to familiarize myself with this boat." She looked at Ethan. "Have you had any experience with a boat like this?"

"Just riding in one," he answered. "Not piloting one. I'm more of a canoe and kayak guy."

The boat had a huge engine in back and four oars.

"Give me a few minutes," Mom said. "You might as well eat something or just chill out."

We broke out the camp stoves and started water boiling. I sat down next to Ethan.

"I don't understand why you came after us," I said.

Ethan smiled. "I told you I wasn't very good at following orders."

"We didn't have orders. We had a plan."

"They figured out we'd flown the coop quicker than we thought. Halfway up the hill, I spotted the guard following us. He was moving quickly, but he was alone. That could only mean that Émile and Géant were going after you. I sent the film crew on ahead and told them to keep going, no matter what. I waited for the guard and ambushed him."

I didn't ask what he meant by "ambushed," because I already had a pretty good idea. I noticed that after Ethan had checked Émile, he hadn't once looked back where he lay. He had done what he had to do, but he wasn't proud of it.

"My choice then was to catch up with the film crew or try to help you. Wasn't much of a choice. I hurried back down to the stream, grabbed my gear, and set out to find you, which wasn't as easy as I thought it would be until I saw the snow leopard."

"The one that got skinned?"

Ethan shook his head. "No, I saw that one later. This one had to be the same one that helped me with the trapdoor. I know you're going to think this is weird, but I think it was leading me to you."

"I don't think that's weird at all."

"Good, because I believe that's exactly what it was doing. I lost your tracks in the woods."

"That's because Zopa and I smudged them out."

"That explains it. When I broke out of the trees onto the plateau, I had no idea where you were. That's when the snow leopard showed up again. It would run in front of me, then stop as if it were waiting up. It seemed crazy to trust a cat, but that's what I did. It led me to the skinned cat. I freaked out. When I first saw it, I thought it was one of you. Anyway, when I was gawking at that horror story, I heard the gunshots."

"They caught up to us just as we reached the gorge."

"That's what I figured. The snow leopard bounded ahead and led me to Géant. Who shot him?"

"Mom."

"From the gorge?"

I nodded.

"Wow. That's good shooting with a pistol at that range. He was probably dead before he hit the ground."

I didn't want to talk about dead people. We'd all had enough of that. "What happened then?"

"I saw the snow leopard disappear over the cliff and start following you down. By the time I got there, you were four hundred feet below. Too long of a shot for me. My only choice was to jump when you got to the bottom and hope for the best. The glide was a little difficult in that narrow space, but there wasn't much wind, so I was able to control it. I was shocked Émile didn't look up. If he had, it would have been dead man falling."

THE RIVER

I think the trick to keeping a boat afloat in fast water is to be faster than the water. As soon as we launch, Mom guns the motor. I'm behind Zopa. Alessia is behind Ethan. We're manning the oars. The problem is, with the exception of Ethan, none of us have ever used an oar.

"Dig in!" Ethan shouts over the roar of the water.

Zopa's oar snaps in two as we slam into the opposite wall of the gorge. My oar stays intact because I'm not strong enough to hold it against the wall. The handle hits me in the chest like a brick. I tumble backward. Mom saves me from going overboard by grabbing a handful of T-shirt and shoving me back into place.

The boat is spinning, bouncing from one side to the other, banging into walls, like a pinball. It's like falling horizontally and trying to save yourself by clutching a wet beach ball. During one of our out-of-control spins, Mom guns the motor just as the bow swings upstream. The boat stabilizes.

"Use the paddles as rudders!" she shouts. "Keep the boat centered! I'll control the speed!"

And in this way, we slowly back our way out of the gorge . . .

AS SOON AS we hit calmer water, we pulled over to shore to bail out the boat and repack our gear. Ethan got on the two-way and tried the film crew. JR answered right away.

"*Where are you?*"

"Upriver from you. Where are you?"

"*Still crossing the scree. We should be at base camp in an hour or so. What about the guard?*"

Ethan hesitated.

"He's not going to be a problem. You're safe. We're all safe."

Not Phillip, or Elham, or Aki, or Choma, or Ebadullah, I thought.

"So you're in a boat?"

"Yeah. We might even get to base camp before you."

WE DID GET TO BASE CAMP before them, but there were people there. Rafe and Cindy were standing outside their tents. They looked as surprised to see us as we were to see them. The camel and the donkey were there as well. Rafe looked even worse than he had two days earlier. The butterflies had come loose. He had a flap of skin hanging down on his forehead.

"You're supposed to be in a kayak halfway to Kabul by now," Ethan said.

"That didn't work out, mate. Hit some rocks. We saw a boat just like this come by. Tried to wave him down. Blighter wouldn't stop. Figured that if there was one boat, there would be more. We decided to come back here and wait for another boat. Someone friendlier."

Ethan grinned and shook his head but said nothing about who the blighter in the boat had been or what he would have done if he had stopped.

"Where'd you get the boat?"

"Long story," Ethan said.

"Where's Phillip?" Cindy asked.

I'd been waiting for this. So had Mom. And Alessia.

"Let's go up to the tent," Mom said. She and Alessia took Cindy's arm and led her away.

"Aki? Choma?" Rafe asked.

We shook our heads. Ethan began explaining what had happened as he patched Rafe up again. I walked down to the river. Zopa joined me. He had a sat phone in his hand.

"There's a signal," he said.

I shrugged.

"I suppose we should wait and have Alessia call the embassy."

"Yeah," I said. "And within a few hours after the call, our camp will be swarming with helicopters filled with soldiers, police, and the press. We'll be an international news story. Plank's Peace Climb will be a disaster."

"Do you care about what happens to Plank?"

"I have never met him, but he was trying to do a good thing. So were Choma, Aki, and even Phillip, in his own way. It's bad enough that Émile and the others murdered our friends. I don't think they should be allowed to murder the Peace Climb as well."

"What do you have in mind?"

I gave him another shrug.

"Tell me."

"It's too crazy. We're all exhausted. Give the phone to Alessia. Let the story begin."

"Whose story is it?" Zopa asked.

"It's our story."

Zopa smiled. "Then let's talk to the other characters and see how they want it to end."

I WAS SHOCKED that Cindy wanted to go with us, and even more surprised when she insisted on climbing. She didn't do too bad, considering that the most complicated thing she had ever climbed was a ladder. I put her in the *P* cave, and I took the *E* cave, so I could keep an eye on her. Rafe climbed up to the *A*, although he said he really didn't want to. Mom took *C*, and Zopa took the last *E*. We spent the night in the caves and climbed down at dawn.

Alessia called the embassy.

We spent the wait keeping the *vautours* off our friends Elham and Ebadullah.

HOLIDAY

PIERRE, WHOSE REAL name was François Bast, was caught three days after we left the French embassy. I'm not sure what happened to him, but I hope he rots away forever in a bastille. The Afghan he was with was not caught. His last known whereabouts were somewhere in Syria. There was not one news report about what happened to us in Wakhan Corridor. The French government wanted to keep it quiet, and so did we.

Sebastian Plank flew to Kabul to meet us as soon as he heard what had happened. He wanted to cancel the Peace Climb and the documentary, but we talked him out of it. It wasn't his fault. It wasn't our fault. The fault lay at the feet of the terrible men who murdered our friends.

JR, Will, and Jack flew to their studio in Boulder, Colorado, to edit their video.

Rafe went back home to Australia, with what I am sure is a very interesting version of what happened on the climb and the role he played in it.

Cindy went back to California to pursue an acting career, and she's gotten a couple of small parts. The reason I know this is because she sends me text messages several times a week. I write her back when I see the texts, which is not very often, because my phone is . . . well, you know.

Ethan decided to stay in Kabul. Alessia's mother hired

him as her security chief, but the real reason he stayed was to learn Pashtun and more about Afghan culture. He couldn't get that snow leopard out of his mind.

"I need to see what I can do about helping those cats," he had said. "The snow leopard was there when we needed it. I'd like to return the favor."

After returning the camel and donkey to their owners, Zopa stuck around long enough to meet Plank and asked him for a lift back to Kathmandu on his private jet. I went to the airport with them to see him off. Just before he stepped into the jetway, I thanked him for everything and told him to say hello to Sun-jo for me.

He put his hand on my shoulder, looked me in the eye, and said, "You ended the story well."

But I guess stories never really end.

Alessia comes into the kitchen, where I'm writing.

"The show is starting."

She and her mother are in New York for the holidays. Alessia is staying with us.

I close the Moleskine journal and follow her into the living room. Rolf and Mom are on the sofa. The two Peas are on the floor with pillows and bowls of popcorn.

"Sit with us, Alessia!" Patrice says.

"Yes, with us!" Paula echoes.

"She doesn't want to lie on the floor," Mom protests.

"No, no," Alessia says. "I would love to lie between the two pea pods."

Patrice turns around just before the documentary starts. "Are we going to the zoo tomorrow to see the shens?"

"*Of course,*" *I answer.*

We have gone almost every day since I returned. The cubs are getting big. We watch them playing in the snow.

The Peace Climb begins. No commercials. Just beautiful climbs on different mountains on the same day all over the world. Patrice keeps turning and asking when our climb will appear. They have no idea what happened to us in After Can Stand.

"*Soon,*" *I tell them.*

Our climb appears at the very end. It is three minutes long.

"*It's a Christmas tree,*" *Patrice says.*

"*No it's not,*" *Paula says.* "*It's a little mountain. It spells* peace.*"

I look at Mom and Alessia. There are tears in their eyes.

There are tears in my eyes.

The letters do not stand for peace, *but I wish there were* peace.

AKI

ELHAM   CHOMA

PHILLIP   EBADULLAH

ACKNOWLEDGMENTS

Books are written in solitude, but published with a great deal of help from hard-working book people. I want to thank Betsy Groban, Scott Magoon, Lisa DiSarro, Hayley Gonnason, and the entire team at HMH, who have stood behind Peak since his climb on Everest in Tibet and now join him on his arduous trek in Afghanistan. Special thanks go to Julie Tibbott who "out of the blue" asked me to write the introduction for the classic Western *Shane* by Jack Schaefer. It was a great honor to be picked to write this introduction, which led me to my old friend, and my fabulous editor, Julia Richardson. If it weren't for Julia, this climb would have never happened.